FORGOTTEN SINS

A DARK MAFIA ROMANCE (NEVER BEEN CAUGHT 2)

IVY WONDER

CONTENTS

Blurb   v

Prologue   1
Chapter 1   7
Chapter 2   11
Chapter 3   16
Chapter 4   22
Chapter 5   29
Chapter 6   37
Chapter 7   43
Chapter 8   50
Chapter 9   55
Chapter 10   59
Chapter 11   64
Chapter 12   71
Chapter 13   81
Chapter 14   86
Chapter 15   93
Epilogue   101

Made in "The United States" by:

Michelle Love

© Copyright 2021

ISBN: 978-1-64808-787-5

🌻 Created with Vellum

BLURB

I woke up in a cute tiny cabin with a splitting headache and no memories.
The sweet, isolated artist who discovered me doesn't know a thing either.
But getting mended by a curvy guardian angel named Eve is a big help.
Especially when I learn about her crush on me.
Still, it's not all roses.
I have a bullet-crease in my skull and skills I can't explain.
When the nightmares start, maybe I'd be better off without those memories?
But the past won't leave me alone.
Whatever happens...I'll make sure they never lay a hand on my petite Eve.

PROLOGUE

Carolyn

Date: January 20, 2018
Location: Boston, Massachusetts
Subject: Michael Di Lorenzo
Criminal Record: Italian national until the age of nineteen; no juvenile records forwarded from Barri PD. Alleged enforcer for the Sixth Family in Montreal, Canada. Suspected in a total of twelve murders of mob members, petty criminals, and as of three weeks ago, Don Gianni Lucca, Don of New York. Three of these murders have occurred on American soil, and Di Lorenzo is currently in the United States.

Suspect was most recently sighted in Boston on January 17 meeting with an unknown individual expected to be a member of the Boston Family. He has not been seen since. It is possible that he is presently targeting Gianni Lucca's eldest son, Carlo, who is currently being held for transfer to New York on racketeering charges.

Given the high probability that an assassination attempt will be made by Di Lorenzo prior to the transfer, the jail facility where he is being held should be staked out with assistance from Boston branch FBI agents and Boston PD.

I open the photo of Michael Di Lorenzo and shudder slightly. He's good looking, but I loathe him. The order to kill Gianni Lucca came down from on high, of course, but it was Di Lorenzo who pulled the trigger.

And in doing so, he ruined my chance of landing a truly high-profile criminal—the Don of freaking New York, no less! That would have been a career-making capture, and my disappointment and anger are still fresh.

If I can catch him now, before he takes out Lucca's son, it will be a big step upward even if his mobster boss is out of reach. I'm tired of profiling and chasing perverts and identity thieves. I want to bring in a killer—and Di Lorenzo is undeniably a killer.

Still, I have to admit, he's a dish. Dark and intense, hair and eyes as black as the coffee in my mug and a lean, solemn face like a Roman patrician's. Tall—a weakness of mine—and gorgeously well-muscled, another weakness.

Holy crap! I definitely need to get laid if my suspects seem sexy!

Di Lorenzo is coincidentally the second one on the list of five never-been-caught suspects that my boss, Derek Daniels, wants me to apprehend within the next four months. It's just that now, there is a personal reason to hunt him down too.

The only problem is that Di Lorenzo is a fucking ghost, and has been since he camouflaged himself as a border guard and gunned down Lucca on his way back to the States. Fake identities, disguises, no prints on file and no news or rumors about him on- or offline. All I can do is watch his target and hope for the best.

I look above my laptop at the window my desk faces. Across the street, the jailhouse looms brutally; a massive concrete gravestone, the surface broken by slit windows. A dozen extra cops and four FBI agents are beefing up security over there, while I sit tight listening to their radio exchanges, and meanwhile shake down every local and internet source I have.

My cellphone buzzes: Daniels again. I hesitate before picking up; he's far better at flinging sarcastic barbs than giving useful instructions or information. "Hello?"

"Catch you napping, Special Agent?" Daniels' voice is already malicious. He's always held a grudge because I won't sleep with him, and silenced him with threats of a formal complaint when he kept whining about it.

"Hardly. Working on my report. No news yet locally." Why is he calling me? He bugs me at least four times a day even if I'm just stuck in a hotel room running searches. It's like he doesn't trust me to do the most basic tasks on my own.

Or maybe he wants to constantly remind me he's watching me? In that case, he can get in line, because ostensibly he's not the only one.

"So, I've gone over your notes from your last case. Looks like you're o for one on the Chase pursuit." His tone is mocking. "He's either still in Montreal or dead."

Alan Chase, car thief turned unlikely hero, is neither, but I don't correct him. Daniels would never understand why the first man on my never-been-caught list was released. But a deal's a deal, and Chase helped me drive the Don back across the American border from Montreal, where we planned to grab him.

It's not Chase's fault that Di Lorenzo ruined things. "Yes sir, I'm quite aware of that. Is there anything else?"

He sounds incredibly amused. "Yes. Lucca's youngest brother Tony made bail and is going to the Berkshires for a ski vacation. Are you guarding the right brother? Because if the Sixth Family's sent Di Lorenzo after all of Lucca's kids—"

I sit back and squeeze my eyes shut. Shit.

Of course Di Lorenzo will go for the unguarded brother. Tons of accidents can happen on a ski slope. "How long have you known?" I demand before stopping myself.

"Half an hour. I've booked you at the same ski resort. A courier should be there in half an hour with everything you need." He's all business now. Assistant Director Daniels is always skirting the edge of things I could formally complain about—but he ducks back into safe territory the moment I actually accuse him of anything. Of course.

Damn it, I could have had a Walter Skinner or a Gordon Cole, or even a Jack Crawford. Instead I ended up with this dick. "Understood, sir. I'll get ready."

"Don't lose this one too, Carolyn." He uses my first name disdainfully and then hangs up.

Back teeth hurting from his disrespect, I pocket my phone and get ready. Not difficult; I never really unpack in a hotel room. Daniels sends me off somewhere else with a moment's notice.

I double check the bathroom for toiletries and jewelry, and get everything together by the door except my coat and laptop case. Then I sit down to send a very important e-mail. Daniels's information and bribery cash may be arriving by courier, but my other big resource is strictly on-line.

I developed an unusual contact while working on the Chase case. He's a hacker of some kind, who keeps e-mailing me. At first he was doing it from temporary phone numbers or e-mails that blocked me when the conversation was done. Now, I have an e-mail address he's been willing to hang onto for more than an hour or so.

He calls himself Prometheus. I have suspicions about who he might be, and they're enough to keep me curious—and invested to keep him talking. He's also been an excellent source a few times.

I address an encrypted e-mail to him and hesitate. His e-mails are always to-the-point. He will probably appreciate it if I communicate the same way.

I need to know everything you know about Michael Di Lorenzo.

The answer comes in under five minutes, while looking up the file on young skiing enthusiast Tony Lucca.

Three things you need to know about Michael Di Lorenzo, Special Agent.

The first is that he started planning to leave the Sixth Family

instantly after the assassination of Gianni Lucca. The second is that his employers are now aware of this fact, and have not responded positively. The third is that a second group of Sixth Family hitters have followed him to the Berkshires and will likely reach him before he reaches Tony Lucca.

"Oh shit." Always complications. The information is reliable; I wouldn't keep going back to Prometheus if it wasn't. But that doesn't make it easy to read.

I respond at once. It won't be long until the courier shows up with **He's in some serious trouble. Think he'll make a deal to get out of it?** If I can find him before the assassins do, this may work out better for me.

The answer, however, is less than reassuring, and contributes to how fast I hurry down to the rental car once the skinny bike courier comes and the goods are in my hands. Prometheus sends just three words—but three words that mean I could be o for two in my list of five before the day's over.

If he survives.

CHAPTER 1

Eve

There's a snowstorm coming this weekend. I'm alone and need to be ready. Several casualties already, making its way across the Midwest, and even though we're only expecting a couple of feet and some ice, better to suppose I won't be making it off the mountain for a few days.

I reassure myself that I can handle this. I have food stores for a month, a high-capacity generator and enough fuel. There's stored water in case the line freezes. Even a snowmobile in case of emergencies, though it will only take me as far as Great Barrington, some fifteen minutes away.

It took me a lot of time, scrimping and saving and selling prints and bags and t-shirts with my art online, and buying things piece by piece so that I never have to face another winter blackout unprepared.

When winter gets treacherous, seclusion can make it worse—and I'm isolated. Nobody in the world knows I'm up here except for a few friends, my single neighbor a quarter mile away, and some shop-keepers and delivery guys. Going for help would be challenging; getting to me if I called for help would be problematic, especially once the snow piles up.

Most of the time, the solitude is worth the risk. The damn anxiety is healing now that I'm giving myself more of a break from people. I can go into town and deal with my fellow humans for hours, even the whole day, because a safe, completely private place awaits me once I'm done.

Times like this, though...Am I a fool for staying here alone?

I come up from my basement, which is my storeroom and the automated center of the house. Everything is checked; everything is ready. No matter what happens, I will be able to sail through it. Just me and my menagerie.

The cottage is almost two hundred years old, built in the Berkshires by a Dutch settler who wasn't interested in being close to a lot of people. The snowfield behind it is my garden three seasons out of the year; now I scatter corn and seeds out onto it daily to feed some creatures and draw them close.

I've always liked the company of animals more than humans, and watching birds and squirrels flock to food in the middle of winter does my heart well. It's easy to win over animals; all you really have to do is be generous, nonviolent, and learn to listen to them. It's not so easy to win over humans.

My family greets me as I walk in: two cats, Loki and Freya, my foul-mouthed adopted parrot Diogenes, and Berry, who is...a special case. He's hanging off the wagon-wheel chandelier as I walk into the room, and chitters at me.

"Hi, Berry. Get off the ceiling, please." The raccoon squeaks and makes grabby-hands at me; I roll my eyes and reach up to give him a lift to the couch.

"How do you even get up there, you fatty?" I don't do wildlife rehabbing, but Berry is unique. I found him on the highway clinging to his road-killed mother, and couldn't just leave him. Fish and Wildlife would be all over me if they knew this.

Another good reason to live alone: I can do what I want.

Berry wanders along the couch while I glance around, trying to figure out if I've forgotten anything. There's enough firewood for a month. The propane tank is full. The storm shutters are sealed, and all my beasts are warm and safe inside.

But the creeping sense of worry has me check things until I realize what I'm doing and stop.

"It's going to be fine," I tell myself firmly.

I've lived on this highland for six years, ever since my mother died and left me enough inheritance to buy the cottage and its half-acre of property. I wouldn't have chosen the Berkshires, but I'm not rich, and a hundred thousand dollars stretches a lot further when you go someplace out of the way.

And I wanted out of the way, even with the risks. Alone, no complications, no abuse. No dreadful mother; no terrible men.

And all the green beauty of nature soothing my eyes and helping to heal my soul.

"Ecce homo!" yells the bird, spreading his bare little chicken wings and bobbing his featherless head. He's in a tiny purple sweater I knitted and clings to a heated perch. Like me, he hasn't had the best life and still deals with symptoms from the stress. Unlike me, he pulls out his feathers habitually instead of compulsively checking the heater, the locks, the windows, and the stove.

The cats are both in loaf mode next to the wood stove, which dominates one side of the room. Berry hops off the couch and ambles over to Loki, who opens one yellow eye and goes from being a chunk of darkness to a cat. Stripy gray Freya rolls on her side and bats a paw at the raccoon. The pair of them are helping to raise Berry, so they're remarkably tolerant as he burrows between them and chatters.

I start to calm down watching them. The aching loneliness inside me is better with their presence; I'd be lonelier around most humans I have met. If anything, my sense of loneliness was worse when I lived in my mother's home, and everyone in my life was bullying me.

It's better to be alone. It means I won't have a lover, it means I won't have a family. But it also means no more abusers, no more bullies, no more people treating me like trash and telling me that I deserve it.

I need a distraction. Music, maybe a movie? "I'll put some tea on," and go for my kettle, filling it and then bringing it to set on top of the wood stove.

A second later, I hear a shuffle outside, followed by a heavy thump.

I pause, frowning. Raccoon? No, too big. There is not enough snow on the roof for it to have slid off and made that sort of noise. So what is it?

Grabbing my fireplace poker, I move toward the door. A soft scraping sound beyond it—and then, to my surprise, a faint groan.

"Shit." I hurry back and pull the insulated curtain that blocks Diogenes' perch from the front door drafts, then open the door and peer out. Am I about to see a drunk or lost tourist? It's twenty degrees out and whoever is out there sounds like they're in pain!

I look out and see a trail of footprints through the snow headed to the door. A larger impression in the snow from a fall. In the moonlight dark spots are visible among the footprints. That's worrisome— but more troublesome is the person who left them.

At my feet, an enormous man in a damaged gortex coat lies unconscious.

CHAPTER 2

Eve

"Is this really happening?" He moves slightly, and I see blood in his dark, wavy hair. He groans again, as if in response to my voice, and I quickly try to sort out how to drag him inside.

It's not like I have any choice. Otherwise there will be a corpse on my porch come morning.

Thinking fast, I roll him over—it takes some effort, he's really heavy—and then grab the bottom of his coat and use it to drag him inside. The tough leather creaks as I grunt and strain, too aware of the icy air flowing into my home. It takes me several seconds of stopping to rest and then heaving backward again, my shoulders cracking from the strain and the cold with every pull.

Finally, I drag him in enough to shut the door, then get him by the pellet stove to warm up. By then my arms are numb with exhaustion. "Damn, what did your mother feed you?" I sigh as I rub my shoulders.

The cats wander over with Berry trailing after them, tails up and ears alert as they investigate the new addition. They sniff delicately at him as I check his condition.

He's pale and battered, perhaps from a car accident; the blood in his hair has mostly dried. He must have seen the lights and come up the mountainside. It's promising that he was able to walk that far; maybe he isn't that hurt. But he's cold and has a head wound, and either one by itself is dangerous enough.

I get his arms out of his coat to check him over. Under the gloves his fingers are cold and his knuckles are bruised. He has some other bruises and a few scrapes. Other than that he's in one piece: no breaks, no big gashes.

The head wound, though, worries me. Especially since he isn't alert yet. I remember from my first aid training that if someone is knocked out for more than a few minutes, they need to get to a hospital. An ambulance might not get up here before the storm hits.

I gingerly touch his head and he flinches, turning it in my direction. Berry jumps back and chatters at him; the cats start grooming their baby to calm him down. Meanwhile, having made sure the blood on my visitor's head isn't still flowing, I'm busy staring at him.

I've seen a lot of attractive men—just not in person. This one, battered, wounded, chilled through and unconscious, is still hot enough to peel the paint off my walls. So much so that I don't know what I'll do when he finally opens his eyes.

Hide, maybe. My cheeks warm just thinking about it. I've never been good around people, and attractive men? Forget it.

And he is gorgeous. Almost startlingly so.

He's got a profile like a Greek marble, a big, solid body, and rugged Mediterranean skin with just a touch of stubble. He even smells nice—sort of. There's an odd sharpness mixed in with the aftershave and leather that stings my nostrils, and smells familiar. I just can't quite place it right now.

Diogenes starts squawking behind his curtain and I reach over and draw it aside again. His little bright blue eyes fix on the new guy and he bobs his head. "Knock knock!"

"Quiet, D, this guy could be in some serious distress." I have no idea who he is, and if I'm going to get him an ambulance, I have to be quick. I check him over carefully, then grab my First Aid kit and some antibacterial wipes to check out his head injury.

The half-dried blood sticks to the wipes, but I manage to clean the wound more or less. It's just a scratch, and though it might scar, it's already scabbing over. Not that bad by itself, but there's a big knot swelling under it, and I'm worried about a concussion.

I know what to do, but I'm not relishing it. Grabbing a penlight off my desk, I crouch next to him and carefully open his eyelids to see if one pupil is larger than the other. Guess those First Aid classes at the Y were actually worth it.

His eyes are so dark a brown that it takes me a moment to tell if one of his pupils is larger—a dangerous sign of bleeding on the brain. He grunts with discomfort each time and his pupils' contract normally. But he doesn't awaken.

"Okay, so you're probably not dying. But who the hell are you?"

I dig into the pockets of his coat hastily, hoping he doesn't think I'm rolling him if he wakes up. I find his wallet and his cellphone, and notice he's wearing a shoulder holster. It's empty, though, and I suddenly realize that smell around him is cordite. Either someone shot at him, or he was shooting back.

What the hell is your story? I wonder looking at his strangely noble face. I want to get out my canvases and paint him, but of course, that's a stupid idea when he's cataleptic on my floor with a bashed head. Instead, I go through the wallet.

There's an issue with it already. One, its stuffed full of hundred dollar bills. Two, there are two ID cards with two different names. David Cahill, and Brian Castello.

I guess immediately that neither one is actually him.

The lack of a legal credential makes the other details more alarming. The guy has an empty holster, smells of cordite, is beaten up, may have a fractured skull from being winged in the head by a bullet, and has a wallet full of cash and fake IDs. None of that is reassuring.

Who are you, mystery guy? Who attacked you? Why are you even on this mountain?

I put his wallet back and try to unlock his phone, but can't. Whatever his unlock code is, it's too complex to guess. I put that back too and see what I can to make him more comfortable on the floor.

As I'm heading upstairs to my bedroom the teakettle starts to whistle. I hurry back and get the tea brewing before putting the kettle back in the kitchen. I see him stir slightly.

"Hey," I start hesitantly. "Hey, can you hear me?"

No answer. At least he's moving around instead of just lying there like log. The color is coming back to his cheeks; he's definitely getting over his chill.

I go get him a pillow and the comforter off my bed, not knowing what else to do. A small, furry entourage follows me from room to room. The animals sense my nervousness and don't want to leave me alone.

Even Diogenes has gone quiet and is staring steadily at the man as I return. I grab a towel from the linen closet before walking into the room and bring it with me as I kneel beside the stranger again.

I cover the pillow with the towel to keep it from getting stains from my half-assed wound cleaning and gently tuck it under his head. I check his pulse and the warmth in his hands; his fingertips are still cool, but his pulse is strong and steady.

"Okay, big guy," I sigh in relief. "Looks like you're going to make it if I get you warmed up. I just wish you would wake up." What am I going to say to him when he does?

I lay the comforter over him on the side facing away from the stove and move away again, going for my tea. But then all I do is cradle it in my hands as it cools, and watch the strange, comatose man.

This isn't my problem! I should just have an ambulance come. Let them deal with whatever this guy is going through. He's been out too long. Even if he looks better, he's still unconscious, and that's a bad sign.

I finally remember to take a swallow of tea, and then reach for my phone. I'm worried that he's got some injury that could kill him.

Except...what if he doesn't want to go anywhere near a hospital?

What if he has people after him, and he doesn't want to go where he could be easily found? Or...

"Oh, shut up, you big nerd," I grumble. This isn't the time to be overthinking issues. He's not waking up, so he needs a hospital.

I pull out my phone and set aside the tea, steeling myself for a tough conversation and an even more difficult visit. I don't really want paramedics or cops in my space, but if that's what is needed right now, I'll deal with it.

I am starting to dial 911 when I notice something and stop, going very still.

The man's eyes are open. And he's staring mutely at me.

CHAPTER 3

Michael

I wake up from red darkness to a room I don't recognize. My head hurts; there's a crease of pain on one side of my skull and the rest throbs dully. But I'm warm, and even though there's a hard surface under me and have no idea what is going on, I'm safe.

At least for the time being.

Someone is moving around near me. I peek through my lashes and see firelight; heat radiates against my side and I'm lying next to a wood stove. There's a pillow under my head and a comforter wrapped around me, and not one but three cats curled up between me and the wood stove. I'm in street clothes, including a leather coat. My boots are on, and my hair feels damp and pasty.

My head feels ready to split open.

A woman is moving around the room, red hair bouncing against her shoulders. She's bundled up in a long green skirt and a demure rose-colored sweater, but the curves of her body push against them rebelliously, refusing to be as modest. Her skin is pale, her manner slightly nervous, and she's standing next to a tall perch with a plucked chicken in a sweater sitting on it.

Hold up a second...

I wonder if I'm dreaming for a few seconds, but the growing discomfort of the hard floor against my side adds to my headache and makes it pretty clear this is the real life. I look around again, baffled; absolutely nothing around me looks familiar.

Then I realize something even worse. Nothing is familiar.

Not the situation, not my clothes, not the wound on my head, not the cats, not the...parrot, I realize, as the creature screeches cheerfully and the woman giggles. I close my eyes again, trying to focus. What was I doing right before I came here?

I feel my stomach tighten as reality settles over me like a cold concrete slab. I'm casting around in my mind for any scrap of memories, where I came from, where I live...what my name is. It's like searching for something in the bottom of a muddy stream; nothing is clear, and everything I grasp under the surface slips away after a moment.

I squash a surge of panic and put everything I have into focusing. What is my name? What do I do for a living? What does my face look like?

Nothing.

Sometimes at the end of each question, I feel a little twitch of reminiscence, but not enough to put anything together. My name is something common; I can remember that much. This is my favorite coat, and I'm worried about it for some reason. When the woman calls the featherless parrot Diogenes, I get the joke.

That's the guy who trolled Plato in front of his students with a plucked chicken after Plato described humans as featherless bipeds. But who told me that? Why do I know it?

I can't remember!

I plow on through the black-red fog inside my mind. Tiny bits of new information surface: a gunshot, shattering glass. Trudging through the blinding cold with my head hurting. The redhead standing over me, a worried expression on her soft-featured face.

Beyond that...nothing clear. Information, knowledge...no personal memories to fully grasp. I know I like beer and am allergic to shellfish. I know Italian language.

My mother's Catholic and she's dead. My father...is another blank spot. What skills do I have? What color are my eyes?

Fuck! This is not a good situation. At least whoever this is cares enough to look after me while I recover from...

...what? How did I get here?

There's only one person to ask: the pretty girl with the gentle gray eyes.

I watch her putter around for a few moments, and then she turns to me and blinks in surprise as she sees my eyes are open.

"Hey there," I manage. My throat feels like I've been gargling sand.

"Oh my God, you're awake! I thought you might not wake up at all." Her musical voice is trembling. Edginess or relief? "Well, I'm awake, but uh..." I push myself up to a sitting position slowly, gritting my teeth against the pain in my head. Two of the cats uncoil; the black one blinks at me and the miniature ticked gray one is a fucking raccoon! "...what the hell?"

"Oh, that's Berry, you're in his spot." She sounds even shakier. She's nervous... Of me?

The third cat, slim and striped, lifts its head and sneezes—then realizes I'm awake and dashes out the door. The other animals are moving away from me, watchful. They don't know me.

"What's your name?" she asks me. She's having trouble with eye contact. Her limbs are pulled in as if she wants to hide.

Not scared. Painfully introverted. And I am a stranger.

"I was kind of hoping you could tell me," I sigh, reaching up gingerly to touch the sore spot on my head. Dried blood, raw skin, and a deep, throbbing ache.

Her jaw drops. "You...you don't know your name?"

I shake my head—and stop at once, wincing. "Ow." Not doing that again for a while.

"Oh, don't do that, you've barely stopped bleeding." She takes a step toward me and hesitates, hands up like she's not sure what the protocol is for dealing with amnesiac strangers on her floor.

"I'll live," I grumble gently, and she blushes, looking away. She's adorable—but tense. Even though I'm the wounded one on the floor. "What's your name?"

"Um, Eve," she replies, still blinking at me like I've sprouted a pair of horns. "You really don't remember anything?"

"Barely. I don't even know how I got up here, or how I got injured." I try to get up and the room tilts sideways.

She hurries forward, bashfulness abandoned, to help me up. She's small and I'm...not, but she still gets her shoulders under my arm and supports me with unexpected strength. She lets out tiny grunts of effort as she helps me over to the broad brown couch, but doesn't quit.

Her hair smells faintly of sweet floral: jasmine? The word comes to me without context as I struggle against a sudden urge to pull her closer. No way is she ready—and I still don't know what the hell is going on.

I flop onto the couch, grunting in discomfort and examine myself. My hands are slightly battered, some random aches and pains, and as I look over the coat, I see something alarming: a fresh bullet hole.

"How long was I out?" I start checking through my pockets. Wallet, keys, cell phone. I feel something under my arm and reach under the coat—an empty shoulder holster.

I stop dead. Why do I have a holster? And where's the gun?

She checks the laptop on the desk behind her. "It couldn't have been more than six minutes. You collapsed on my porch and I pulled you inside."

Six minutes. "That's not too bad."

"I was getting worried. How are you feeling? I was about to call an ambulance." She bends down to scoop up the raccoon, who is pawing at her leg, and I get a peak of cleavage. The skin of her breasts is so smooth that it gleams.

Damn.

"Well, I got a whack on my head, a drum corps practicing inside and no recollections. Other than that I'm fine." I frown. "Glad you didn't call an ambulance, though."

"Huh?" She sits at her desk, kitty-corner to me, still cradling the fur ball like it's a baby. It doesn't seem to mind, either.

"It wouldn´t be the best idea. There's a bullet hole in my coat and I may have been winged in the head too." I investigate the wound again and then force myself to put my hand back down. "Whoever did this probably isn't on the right side of the law and might be looking for me."

She pales. "We're in the middle of nowhere out here."

"Where is 'here'?" This is obviously a cabin; if she's got a baby raccoon just chilling with her we're probably up in the woods somewhere.

"Berkshires. We're about a mile from the highway, all uphill. And there's a snowstorm coming." She's tender worry and reticence, charming me more by the second. "Do you want to call the police?"

"No," I say so quickly that it startles even me. "I don't even know what to tell them yet." But there's something else behind my refusal: abrupt, inexplicable alarm. Whoever I am, and however I ended up shot at and knocked out on a Massachusetts mountainside, I'm probably not the kind of guy who wants to get up close and personal with the cops.

And that's cause for concern.

"What do you want to do?" she asks, quietly. "I'm not used to company outside of the beasts, but you're wounded, and the storm has a wind chill of thirty below."

My eyebrows go up. "Damn. Can you draw aside one of those window quilts and let me take a look outside?"

She nods and goes to the broad front window, which is covered by a heavy, quilted cloth sealed to its frame with Velcro. She unseals it with a ripping sound that sets the parrot to flap excitedly.

"What the hell happened to your parrot?" I ask as she carefully unfastens the window quilt. The bird eyes me, tilting his head.

"Um, he was in a bad circumstance before I got him, and he started pulling out his feathers. Once he is less stressed I'm hoping to get him out of the habit. He's got some feathers under the sweater, but he´s still rather bare right now." She rolls up the bottom of the quilt to expose the window and I can't help but stare.

A steep, forested slope with a single, staggering set of footsteps meandering up the hill through the snow. Fresh snow's already starting to come down, tiny flakes sparkling as they blow past. A single plowed road making its way down the hill from the cabin, on the opposite side from my footprints. "You have a vehicle?"

"Jeep and a snowmobile. I wouldn't drive either in this unless you were still unconscious, though." She peers out at the intensifying storm. "If you want to stay, we'll manage. If you want to get out though, now would probably be the time."

I consider it as I look at that desolate set of footprints. Whoever did this to me, I got away from them somehow. If they didn't follow my trail to the house before the snow started covering it, they were going to have a heck of a time finding me now.

I open the wallet, look at the wad of cash and the two sets of IDs in there, and close it again, leaning back into the couch and shut my eyes. Neither one of the names in my wallet is mine. When I check the phone, I can't remember the unlock code.

She covers the window, and my gaze traces over her: timid, cute, vulnerable and compassionate, with a body I'm already itching to run my hands over. Maybe I can do something about her solitude for a while?

And really, maybe stay put until I have an idea of what is going on? Whoever tried to shoot me might still be looking for me. Waiting out until the storm's over will give me the chance to unearth enough memories.

"I'd like to stay for a few days, if that's all right," I reply, and she nods, offering a miniscule smile.

CHAPTER 4

Eve

He's an amnesiac, and someone tried to kill him.

I feel like I'm in a spy movie.

I am also having such a massive attack of self-consciousness that I've started puttering around straightening the living room until he coughs politely and I stop to look his way with a throw pillow in one hand.

"You know, you dragged me out of the deadly cold and are letting me stay in your home. You don't have to straighten up for me too." His smile melts through my edginess like sunlight on snow.

I blush and set the pillow down. "It's just been a while," I murmur, cheeks still hot. I can't look at him long; he can see me staring, and so I glance away quickly between small eye contact.

He's too handsome! What could happen if he realizes I can't take my eyes off of him? Good-looking men can be the cruelest. Staring into his bright, coal-black eyes is like staring into the sun; I can't look too long or it starts hurting.

No man has ever touched me. Of course, I haven't been trying to date for the last six years. But before then, in my awkward teens, rejection was day in and day out.

Now, I'm sitting across from a man I already wish would touch me, who is in my home and has every reason to look kindly on me for saving him. And I'm still so nervous I can barely breathe!

"What should I call you?" I ask, spending my nervous energy making tea for us instead. Berry is still following me around, hiding behind my legs and peeking at the newcomer, who is more intimidating now that he's awake.

"I'm still hoping that I'll remember soon." He offers a lopsided, wry grin. "That and my phone's unlock code." He's sitting more upright, his expression more alert. "Thanks for this."

How to respond to that? Would I be so eager to welcome him if it wasn't an emergency, no matter how hot he is? Alone means safe, and I don't give up my safety easily.

Except...look at him! He looks like a wounded Roman god. I could sit here painting him all day long! The only reason it would look bad would be if I couldn't stop my hands from shaking.

I make a small noise of acknowledgment and bring him his mug after dropping a dollop of honey into the tea. "You're sure you don't want a doctor to check you out?"

"No, it's not worth the risk of driving. Besides, now that I'm warming up I don't feel so shitty. I probably collapsed from the cold." He has a slight accent: Spanish maybe?

He takes the mug; our fingers brush and I almost drop it before he gets a good grip.

"Oh, sorry," I mumble and he just smiles and shakes his head.

"You're really not used to other people in your space, are you?"

That sends a shiver through me as memories loom. I push them aside. At least I have memories, even if most of them are crappy. "I uh...moved up here for an intention."

Those days are well behind me now, and I'm frustrated that that same jitters keep seizing me in spite of that.

"I see. Then you are going out of your way for me." His deep, warm voice is tinged with regret, and I hastily shake my head.

"I couldn't live with myself if I just left you freeze, or tossed you out in the cold now." One of my ways of living with myself is to be better than my abusers. Even if it means that I now have a hefty stranger in my house who may have recently been in a gunfight.

That is weird to think about, especially since I don't know the context. Is he an undercover cop? That would make sense, though an extra set of ID under a different name in his wallet doesn't.

In a way, it's a comfort he knows as little as I do. Unless of course he's lying...it wouldn't be the first time a man has lied to me. But somehow I don't think so. Maybe it's the worry haunting the back of those deep black eyes?

"Well, I'm lucky as hell to have found a kind person in the middle of nowhere. Probably one of the few benevolent people around here." His eyes twinkle at me and I look away quickly, taking a scalding gulp of tea.

"Not everyone here is that bad." In small doses, anyway. "They mostly keep to themselves except for the tourists going to the ski lodge."

He pauses briefly in bringing his tea mug to his lips and his brows furrow. "Ski lodge?"

"Yes, it's uh...one of the biggest moneymakers in the area. Why?" His whole body has tensed. "Are you remembering something?"

"...maybe. It's too vague." He mutters something unintelligible in a frustrated voice. "I just hope this memory loss is as temporary as my blackout."

"You should probably go get an MRI once the storm's over." Am I being too pushy? He simply nods.

"Yeah, I have to make sure there's no permanent damage. I seem to be recovering quickly, though. This is good," he says before taking another swallow of tea.

"It's green tea with dried mango bits. I thought tea with honey would help." My cheeks are warming up again. He said thank you. He likes tea. Maybe he will like me.

Then I get exasperated. What are you doing? Focus!

"Well, you were right." He drains the rest of his tea. Except for the dried blood in his hair, he almost looks like a guest instead of someone who collapsed on my porch. "I am feeling better. I can probably stand up by myself now."

"Would you um, like to get cleaned up?" I ask hesitantly. That mess in his hair doesn't look comfortable.

He perks up. "Yeah, a hot shower would help in a lot of ways. Maybe I can even remember some more things. Some of my best thinking is in the shower."

"At least it helped you remember that," I joke lamely, and he chuckles. I still wonder if he's playing with me.

"It's weird," he murmurs, frowning as he levers himself to his feet and sets his cup down on the heavy timber coffee table. "It's not so much that things are missing as that they're obscured. Like when you try to remember something from a long time ago, but the details keep slipping away."

"I don't know how amnesia works," I admit. "But you don't seem confused otherwise."

"I was at first. I must have been walking up that hill a while those footprints." He pauses and grins awkwardly. "Uh, I guess they're covered now."

I hide a smile behind my hand. "I saw them. You were just staggering around. I wish I had seen you out there sooner."

"You were there when I needed you, and that's enough," he cut in as he took off his coat. I stepped forward to take it, and something fell out of his pockets and pattered on the floor. Glass cubes, edged in blue-green—safety glass from a shattered windshield.

"Car accident," he says suddenly, brow furrowed again. "That was part of it."

"It's probably a hopeful sign that your memory is returning this soon, anyway," I reassure while wondering what situation he survived.

"I suppose. What the hell will I find out about myself? So, where's the bathroom?"

I take the towel off the pillow and hand it to him, then put the pillow and comforter on the couch for later. "Down the hall, left side."

He nods and shoulders the towel before walking down the hall. Watching him go—his tight ass and muscular back accentuated by a clinging sweater and well-tailored trousers—leave me gaping until he turns to the bathroom door and out of sight—followed by Freya, who meows at him. "Hey cat. Going to watch me shower? Furry perv."

I'd watch too, I think—and immediately blush harder than ever. Oh my God, listen to me!

Why did he have to be this hot? I could handle this better if he was an ordinary guy. But this is the situation, and it needs to be handled without making a complete idiot of myself.

First things first. I go over to my laptop and look up amnesia. Symptoms, indications, causes. I skim a Mayo Clinic article and frown.

Two types of amnesia: the sort that affects past memories and the sort that keeps you from making new ones. A temporary amnesia fades in hours, another can diminish within a few days to a few weeks. Then there's permanent or semi-permanent amnesia.

The causes vary. Brain disease, tumors, concussion, and psychological trauma.

Like getting shot at, getting into a car accident and nearly dying. He's a tough guy, but nobody's that tough.

I would be a complete mess if I went through someone trying to kill me. If it wasn't for the IDs, I would wonder if he was a victim of road rage. They happen all over, especially when the weather's bad.

We'll find out eventually. I just hope we can put this guy in touch with his family. They must be worried sick.

Interestingly, he's not wearing a wedding ring. But he must have a girlfriend... Guys like that are only single if they want to be. My heart sinks at the idea...but I need to keep it in mind.

Stay objective!

The water turns off; about a minute later the door opens and he leans out of the doorway. "Hey," he says. "Hair dryer?"

He's half naked as he leans out the bathroom door, his skin gleaming. My eyes widen. Oh shit!

I've actually never seen an unclothed guy before, not in person. Let alone one who's so fine-looking that I've been drinking him in every single time he's not looking. Now, there's a lot more to drink in... And it takes all my strength of will not to stare.

His skin gleams in the light. I see a few scars, including one next to his navel, but it's barely noticeable compared to the rest of him. A few droplets of water cling to his olive skin like jewels, and trace slowly down the slope of his chest, then bounce down his rippled belly to catch in the traces of hair below his navel. My gaze follows them greedily until I catch myself and look back up to his face.

"Um..." Holy shit. Okay. Keep it together, Eve. "Sorry, I had it in here for craft stuff." I fetch it off my art table, heart pounding in my ears and my face prickling with heat. And not just my face.

Sexual desire has always meant sexual frustration to me. Between the inhibition, the abuse and being curvier than most teenage boys like, I couldn't even approach guys who made me weak in the knees. The cruel teasing would have simply intensified.

I've tried to ignore my frustrated desire like I've tried to ignore my loneliness. But as I look at him, a sharp, almost painful tingle runs through me, centered on my pussy. I almost want to tell him to come over here so I can dry him off with body heat, but I don't have the nerve.

Instead, I hand him the hair dryer and he turns to disappear in the bathroom, giving me an even better view of his posterior. I bite my lip, staring, now that his back's to me. The door closes, and I let my breath out, shaking my head.

Stop. You know nothing about this man—he knows nothing about himself. And you have no idea how to flirt anyway. Don't make this even stroppier.

I busy myself feeding Diogenes, checking the progress of the storm (the footprints really have vanished) and playing with Berry, who keeps bringing me his jingle ball to throw for him and the cats.

A good three-way game of chase-the-ball was under way when the bathroom door creaks open again.

My visitor comes out shirtless, pants and boots on, the rest of his clothes in his hands. "Hey," he says with an innocent smile. "Do you have anything to eat around here?"

Oof. I smile awkwardly and nod, turning to the kitchen. "Plenty. Come on."

How will I get a wink of sleep with this unbelievably hot mystery man around?

CHAPTER 5

Michael

In the shower, I discovered a lot of scars. Old and new, mostly trivial, some of them suspect-looking. A small sun in scar tissue on either side of my right thigh, alarmingly high up and close to the family jewels. A thin, twisted scar next to my navel. Some other long, thin scars on my forearms, and one across my lower back.

I touch the sunburst-shaped ones as the water slowly washes dried blood out of my hair, and something in my rattled brain fires properly. For a moment, I hear a gunshot, and then a hard impact on my leg, like someone just punched me. I look down and am surprised to see blood.

Then I blink, and it goes away, and I'm looking at a scar again. This is a gunshot wound. Someone tried to cripple me—or castrate me—long ago. Now, I don't even feel a twinge from it.

I run my finger over the scar by my navel and another flashback happens. This one is gut-churning pain as a knife thuds into me. The thought I was on antibiotics for three months comes to my head, and then that goes away too.

I've been in a lot of fights. Am I a soldier? A cop? A mercenary? A crook?

Why the hell can't I remember?

Still, Eve is right; I am recalling things swiftly. Maybe it's the fact that I'm finally warm, and well away from danger? The source won't come back outside of those few images, no matter how hard I try.

I wash my hair very carefully, the hot water and soap stinging my scalp. No bleeding, but the water from my scalp goes from almost sludgy brown to tea-colored over the course of minutes and still takes a while to get clean. Meanwhile, the throbbing in my head carries on unchanged, and the lump under the wound got big.

Fortunately, the wound didn't {t bleed again. Whatever happened rattled my brains but didn't jeopardize my life. Except of course losing consciousness in the middle of an icy woods.

I'm just glad it happened on such a kind and lovely woman's doorway.

Eve. She's adorable and exactly my type. Even in her frumpy clothes I noticed that while realizing I have amnesia.

And she's lonesome. Desperately so. What kind of trauma has made her isolate herself in a cottage out in the woods? It doesn't change the fact that she longs for company. The small collection of creatures she babies is proof enough.

Maybe I can do something about that? I already like her, after all, and she deserves a nice thank-you for saving my life. I smile as I rinse out my hair a final time and give myself another look-over.

Whoever I am likes to keep fit, and not just for utility. The manscaping makes that clear, along with the moisturized skin. The guy likes appealing to women, especially with his clothes off.

No wedding ring, no tan lines. No pictures of a lady in that strangely plain wallet. How to unlock the damn phone? Maybe if I wait long enough the unlock code will come back to me?

It's odd how with a bullet crease in my skull, broken glass in my coat pocket and no idea of who might be after me, I'm making sure that I'm not already involved to seduce a young lady I barely know.

Still, it does make for a pleasant distraction from all the unknowns.

I towel off as best I can and poke through the small, pink-tiled bathroom for a hair dryer. Checking every cabinet and drawer ´nothing. Hmm.

Wrapping the towel around my hips so I won't give my host an unexpected eyeful of dick, I go to the door, stepping around the stripy cat, who merps at me but avoids rubbing against my damp leg. "Hey, cat." I nudge her aside with my foot, open the door and lean out.

Eve's expression when her eyes skim over me tells me volumes. It's flattering; as her gaze dips past my navel I feel my cock stir behind the towel. Her eyes widen and she quickly looks away, hurrying to grab the blow dryer off her cluttered art desk.

I hold my laughter until I'm back in the bathroom and the whir of the blow dryer covers my soft chuckles. Someone's got a crush. That's just fucking charming.

Problem is, it's left me with a boner that I could hang the towel on.

As I dry my hair, I think about the walk through the snow, trying to remember how the cold settled into my bones. Nothing surfaces. Just frustration, and my growing exhaustion. At least the boner is going away; I need to fit back into my pants!

I peel the quilt from the single window and look out onto near blank, swirling whiteness. The storm has really picked up. My footprints are gone, my trail buried.

Anyone who tried to follow me is probably lost in this blizzard if they didn't give up and go home. I'm definitely safe here, at least as long as the storm lasts. I should ask about the forecast.

I put my pants and boots back on, grab the rest of my stuff and walk out—only to be greeted by another big-eyed look from Eve. Damn, girl, have you never seen a shirtless guy?

She's probably a virgin! She doesn't know what to say or do when she sees me disrobed. We chat casually for a moment; I mention food, and she leads me to her kitchen. I drop my jacket on the sofa and put my shirt on before following.

"How long is this snowstorm supposed to last?" I ask as she walks to a crock pot steaming away on one of the wood counters.

"Thirty-six hours, plus another twelve-odd before the roads are clear. Why?" She pulls a pair of stoneware bowls out of a cabinet, and starts filling them up with pleasant-smelling stew.

"Just trying to find out how long my reprieve is." I give her a smile in return for the bowl and spoon, and sit down at the small spool table across from the stove.

"Two days, unless they're Bond villains and go after you on skis and snowmobiles. Then a day and a half." She's trying to joke; I chuckle, deliberately pretending not to notice the peeks she's sneaking at me.

"That should give me some lead time. Not to mention a chance to recover... So, since I don't know shit about myself, tell me about you."

"Oh, I uh..." She settles into her seat carefully, and takes up her spoon, then sets it down again. "Well, I'm an artist. I came up here to work. I'm from Portland, Maine, originally." She sits rigidly, manner and expression uneasy.

I take a bite of the stew to give her a moment, chewing and swallowing. It's good—surprisingly spicy enough.

"I went to Boston for art school and wanted to stay." She pokes at the stew with a spoon. "Didn't...really have anything to go back for."

"Is Portland that shitty?" I have no memories of Maine. Stephen King lives there, but know nothing else.

"It...was for me." She winces, and takes a tiny bite. "Nothing life-threatening, but...it was every day."

"What do you mean?" I ask softly.

"Everybody. Family, kids at school, other people. They just...didn't like me," she sighs. "And they had various ways of letting me know."

There's a whole lot of hellish shit involved that she's not telling me about. She probably doesn't want to seem like a whiner in front of a guy with no memories and a bullet crease in his skull.

"Is this a difficult subject?" It may in fact be demanding to have a guest.

Whoever I am seems good at picking up little details about people. Maybe I have a psychology degree? Or am an investigator?

This is like staring at a table full of puzzle pieces and seeing bits of the picture in them, but not what fits where. I can recognize more of the pieces, but it's still baffling and infuriating.

"I'm okay," Eve replies staunchly, but she's not. "Anyway...Portland wasn't a good place to be for me. Too many bad memories."

I hear a chitter, and she shifts slightly; Berry is clambering up her skirt to get into her lap. "I'm sure it's not anything you deserved," I say as the raccoon pops his head up above the table top, nose wiggling in the direction of the stew.

"No, it wasn't," she smiles as she pets the raccoon. "But people like that don't need reasons. They just need excuses."

Somehow that seems terribly familiar. The dismay that creeps into my guts is deeper and uglier than bullies or even abuse could account for. I'm sensing she's hiding something truly awful. Or is she just a sensitive soul and one of the ugliest memory is looming out of the fog?

"I understand. So how did you get into art, anyway?" I fight a smile as she moves her bowl out of the reach of grabby raccoon paws.

"Growing up, in my daydreams, I made up countries, creatures, all sorts of stuff. I just started painting them, from about age ten up." That reluctant flicker of a smile again.

"That sounds cool. After dinner, I'd like a look." I take a bite of stew as she nods.

"Um, no problem." A creeping look of surprise on her face, as if she's starting to realize I'm actually interested.

She is definitely a virgin. Intriguing.

I shouldn't push her into anything. Go slow. But the more I think about it, the more I want to seduce her.

Heck, right now, I'd just like to give her a hug. She seems so kicked around by life, even if things are decent now.

"The stew's really good. Is this mutton?" It has enough garlic that I can't tell which slightly gamey meat it is.

"Venison. One of my neighbors trades me for mail-order stuff during hunting season. The mushrooms are store-bought, though. My foraging skills are not the greatest."

She takes another small bite of the soup, as if hesitant to eat in front of me. "I looked up details on amnesia while you were showering."

I put my spoon down, interested. "Yeah?"

"Your pupils are the same size, and you don't show signs of a concussion. But concussion is one of the causes. I'm guessing that the milder the concussion is the milder the amnesia, but I'm not a doctor."

"Hm." I take another bite of stew while she sips the remnants of her tea. "What are the other possible causes?"

"Drugs, brain infection, tumor, and, um...trauma." She blushes slightly, pale skin turning a delicate pink. "Like PTSD level trauma."

"That last one does not describe me very well," I chuckle...but then that cold feeling in the pit of my stomach and the headache give me a fresh reminder.

There's something in my past that will probably keep me up nights when I remember it. Not knowing what it is bothers me a lot.

"We should take you to the urgent care center when the storm's over." She's stuck on that. But she's worried—genuinely, even though she just met me.

It warms my heart—and my loins. "You've brought that up twice now. I'm guessing your research put a scare into you?" I give her a lopsided smile.

"Yes, I'm following their recommendations as well as my instincts. I can get you there once the road's back open." She talks quickly, embarrassed by her caring.

"Okay. You're right. I'll go with you and get it checked out when we can." I go back to eating. The taste of the stew has reminded me I'm actually ravenous; I couldn't feel it before over the pain. I shovel it in as fast as I can without being vulgar or getting it on my clothes.

"Okay then." She smiles with relief and I nod to myself. She really does have that big of a heart.

And once again, all I can think about as I look into her gentle gray eyes is making them widen with amazed pleasure as she lies under me. Pressing down on my boner underneath the table, I change the subject. "How did you end up with a raccoon?"

"He was on the road next to his dead mother when he was a baby, so I took him and bottle-fed him until he could eat solid food." The raccoon peeks back over the edge of the table from her lap, and she pets his fuzzy head before gently but decisively pushing him back out of sight.

"And the cats?"

"Rescues, like the parrot. I like animals. If I could deal with people I would probably have become a vet." She nibbles at her stew, as if forcing herself to slow down and take tiny little sips. "I guess you wouldn't know if you have pets."

"No, I don't think I do. Otherwise I would probably be more worried. Are they trained?" Another bite of stew. Every spoonful is nourishing.

"Uh, well, Diogenes knows some Greek and can swear in five languages," she starts, and I interrupt with genuine laughter.

"Where did you rescue him from, a multicultural band of jewel thieves?" I watch the raccoon play peek-a-boo with me over the edge of the table and almost miss as Eve's smile fades away again.

"He was, um, in a bad situation, like me," she says very simply. I nod and after a moment, she goes on. "My animals...we all kind of rescued each other. I got them out of bad situations, and they keep me from getting depressed again. And the cats have been raising Berry as much as I have."

"Any human friends?" Her isolation rattles me now that I understand how much of it comes from hiding from harm.

"I'm friendly with a few people in town."

"But not friends. Not really." She's pretty, smart, sweet and kind, and she has interesting hobbies. What is there not to like?

"No," she murmurs. "Some people I thought were my friends, but it didn't work out." The hurt in her eyes deepens and I suddenly want to find whoever hurt her and—

—and what?

Fucking shoot them!

I sit back wide-eyed, blinking down at the tabletop, and she asks immediately, "What's wrong?"

"Nothing," I reply hastily. "I just think you've been living around a bunch of really shitty people." What was that?

The idea of doing violence to the people who had hurt Eve came completely naturally, with neither remorse nor restraint. What kind of man am I?

"Anyway, if you need a friend, you've proven you'll be a good one. So I'm game." Though I have no intention of just being a friend, I don't want to start flirting until I know she's into it. Otherwise, friends it is.

In response, Eve gives me the first real smile that I've seen and my worry melts away in its light.

CHAPTER 6

Michael

"You can't walk away from a job like this, Mikey." The voice echoes toward me as if down a long tunnel. It's male, deep, has a French accent. No, that's not right, not French —Quebecois.

"I'm done, Bertrand. It's enough. I told the Boss no kids." I'm furious; offended. I also have a gun pointed at me. I stare down the bore defiantly.

"If the Boss says you do kids, you do kids. His mommy ran out on us, she knew what the price would be. Now we've got to get rid of him. He's up at the ski lodge with his daddy, same one as Lucca." The man's face is a frustrating blur; he stinks of cigars and wine.

"And what are you going to do if I don't?" I demand, betrayal digging its nails into my heart. This man is a friend. He was my handler for the original. But he was damn quick to pull a gun on me when I declined what he keeps calling a "side job".

"So what? We don't shoot her because the Boss wants her dragged back to fuck for him? We kill an innocent kid instead?" I feel like throwing up. That same disgust that haunted me briefly at the dinner table overwhelms me now.

"That's exactly right. I'm going to collect her while you put a bullet in the kid. Make it quick, Mikey, but I swear to God if you back out I'll put a bullet in you right now." His face is coming into focus: squarish, dark, jowly. His eyes are a dull hazel.

"After ten fucking years, Bertie, you're going to gun me down because I won't shoot a kid? Christ." I laugh bitterly, shaking my head. "You're a piece of work."

"Look, it's not my call." A faint flicker of doubt in his eyes, but that gun still stares me down steadily. "You're his best hitter. If anyone can handle this quick and quiet—"

I take a deep breath, hands flexing, ignoring the holstered gun under my arm. I can't pull it in time.

I don't have to.

"Put away the gun, Bertrand, let's talk. You know what happens to people who hold guns on me." Why I am not scared of that yawning gun bore? One wiggle of his finger and it will spit death out into my forehead—but mostly, his pointing it at me is pissing me off.

"No, don't try any shit with me." His lips twist. "I got my orders, Mikey!"

I lash out at once—striking his gun hand aside and sending its bullet into a tree behind me. Then I snatch the pistol out of his hand and turn it on him.

Bertrand blinks in fear down the barrel of his own gun as I straighten up. "And now you have new orders," I growl. "Get rid of your backup. Slowly."

He swallows, going pale under his dark half-Algerian skin, and then crouches to pull his .38 from his ankle holster. I can see around us now: a stretch of woods, snow on the ground. Very familiar.

"Don't do anything crazy now, Mikey," he breathes in a shivery voice. It disgusts me even more, and when he sees my scowl deepen his eyes widen in alarm. "Oh come on, aren't we friends?"

"We weren't twenty seconds ago," I remind him, and he looks ready to piss himself as he tosses the .38 into the snow. It lands at the base of a lightning-split tree and sinks out of sight.

I press the muzzle to his forehead and he starts to sweat in the cold. "Walk," I request.

"What are you going to do to me?" he asks as he turns to walk into the woods.

I smack him across the head with the barrel and he collapses limply, the snow breaking his fall. I fish for his cellphone, and stuff it inside my coat next to my own. Now he won't get help without walking to town.

"Bye Bertie," I sigh as I turn to walk back to my car. The .44 goes into a pocket as I anger claws at me even more. "It's been real."

Ten fucking years of being best friends, and then he tries to force me to murder a kid as a fucking side job! He knows I have a code. He's stood up for me having one before. What changed?

Part of me wants to shoot him. But the same part of me that made me refuse a job after more than a decade keeps me from pulling the trigger.

I drive away instead.

Bertie doesn't know I've been planning this for months. The hit on a kid was the last straw. I'm staying in the States, leaving Montreal behind.

With six million dollars socked away after ten years of work, I have the few personal things I want to keep. The posh condo with its ornamental furniture and artwork can burn for all I care.

My freedom is worth far more.

I'm deep in the Berkshires, along the same highway, when I realize too late that I should have shot Bertrand through the head after all. I know it for sure when two dark figures step out into the road a quarter mile ahead and aim their guns at me. I stomp on the accelerator as they open fire—

I gasp awake on Eve's couch and sit up fast—sending a jolt of pain through my head. "Ow, fuck," I mutter, barely remembering not to grab for the spot in time.

A dream. Just a dream. Except...somehow, it's not. I was shot at by men stepping out into the road while I was behind the wheel of my car. I must have gotten my injury when a bullet passed through the windshield. Then came the crash...a collision I can't remember, but know that's what must have happened.

And my name. Michael.

And my job.

I'm a fucking hit man! They wanted to kill me when I tried to leave.

That can't be real! That was like something out of a Brian DE Palma movie. Nobody actually lives their life like that.

Do they?

Shuddering, I close my eyes in the dark and try to focus. Some details of the dream are already slipping away.

Maybe it was metaphorical? Maybe it has nothing to do with reality, and I'm just having messed up dreams because I was whacked in the head?

I start to calm down, ignoring the strange sense of certainty that my dream was factual. I'm still waking up after all. Right now my brain will try to fill up the gaps in my recollection with any improbability it can.

I hope.

I look around the warm room, seeing the silhouettes of furniture, the pellet stove and the sleeping parrot on his perch in the faint orange glow from the grate. Whatever that was, it's left me chilled, and hoping it wasn't a precise memory.

A creak of the stairs and I look up to see a curvy figure in a bright gown coming down, her face a blur in the dark. "Are you okay?" she asks tenderly as she hurries the rest of the way.

"Nightmare," I grumble, holding my temple. The quilt has puddled at my waist, exposing my bare chest and shoulders. I shiver a bit and pull it back up.

She comes over, opens up the stove grate and shoves in a few more pellets. "Sorry, do you need a painkiller?"

"It might help."

She goes to the bathroom and comes back with a basket of pill bottles. Setting it on the end of the couch, she opens it and starts poking through by feel. .

She checks labels by the firelight. "Multivitamin, no...CoQ10, no... Prescription strength ibuprofen, there you go."

I open the container and spill two pills, dry-swallow them while she grabs another bottle and takes a pill from it. "Thanks. How did you know?" I'm noticing a lot of stiffness, aches and pains.

"Injuries hurt the worst the day after you get them," she says so casually that I wonder again who hurt her, and how badly. "You may be a tough guy, but you still need to get your rest."

"I know." I give her a thin smile and hand back the bottle. "Sorry I woke you."

"You didn't. I was coming down for a sleeping pill anyway." She sounds confused; she's not used to people apologizing.

"What time is it?" I ask.

"Clock said a little after four." She crosses to the window and peels aside one corner of the window quilt; her gasp sends me to my feet.

"What is it?" I lean in behind her and check for myself.

The storm is still raging, swirls of snow coming onto the porch and piling up in heavy drifts. Beyond it, the snow has risen in windswept mounds. "That's a lot more than two feet," I breathe. "How long is the blizzard supposed to last?"

"At least another day," she sighs. "Looks like we'll need the snow-mobile to get you into town."

"Yeah, looks like." In a way, it's a relief. If my dream is real, then the men who are looking for me are daring indeed. Having extra time to heal up before facing them is good.

She turns around—and stops short, almost bumping into me. She let out a shivery breath, I'm not only half-naked this time, but really close to her. She doesn't tense up or say anything. Good sign.

"If we're spending the next day or so together," she breathes in a trembled voice that sends a tingle through me, "I need to have something to call you."

A tendril of her deep red hair has escaped her braid and lies across her cheek. I reach over deliberately and tuck it behind her ear while she catches her breath.

"Michael," I tell her, brushing her earlobe with my finger before drawing my hand back. "Call me Michael."

CHAPTER 7

Eve

He wants me to call him Michael.

It's apt, with his nearly angelic looks. The guy looks like he could both do a photo shoot for a high end modeling agency and bash someone's face in. All that rippling muscle not two feet away looks good; the heat rolling off of his body feels good. His size is intimidating.

Yet his touch is so gentle.

Trembling, I nod and he backs off, going to the couch. "Try to get some sleep," he suggests. "If I make noise down here, just ignore it. I'll tell you if there's an actual problem. I'm having no difficulty walking anymore."

"That's good," I breathe, unable to stop smiling. "I understand. More sleep."

"Good idea. Don't exhaust yourself—especially on my account."

Back in the bedroom, though, I put my hand over the place where he touched me and feel a tickle rush through me. He was flirting. Only minutely, but he most definitely was.

He likes me. And amazingly...he wants me.

A handful of men acted engrossed by me before, but not in a pleasant way. More in a follow around, harass, grab a boob way. But a gentle man? A man that I can actually like back?

Impossible! Unheard of. Before now, anyway.

A wave of giddiness hits as I bundle myself into bed. Enigmatic Michael might have a shadowy past, but...I don't care!

I like him. He likes me back. He's not a bad person.

This has never happened to me before.

Boys make fun of me. Men ignore me. That's how it's always been.

Now, here's Michael, and he's doing neither. He might be playing me; seeking comfort in his own ambiguous circumstances. But he's positively amazing, and I undeniably spend the next ten minutes fantasizing of kissing him.

Which makes it even tougher to drift off to sleep afterward. Instead, I just lie there, staring at the beamed ceiling, and brush a hand slowly over my belly, wondering what it would be like if I invited him upstairs.

What would he do? How would it feel?

I imagine his sleek, strong body braced against mine, nude, shuddering with lust. I barely manage anything like it, feeling more of that delightful giddiness in place of any kind of physical pleasure.

Oh wow. That's...this is just...

I smile into my pillow, giggling silently, my skin tingling and my whole body warm. The snowstorm outside is a minor inconvenience. His shadowy past and tentative future? Nothing we can't handle.

I wonder what his mouth tastes like, what his dick feels like. And then I'm blushing furiously and giggling again.

This is incredible. I'm so happy just from that tiny touch that I can't imagine anything ruining my mood. I finally drift off as the pill kicks in, smiling the whole time.

"You're getting fat again, Evie. Start skipping breakfast." My mother sits across the table, flabby arms folded as she looks at me in disgust. Next to her, my older sister Melody smirks.

I look at my deplorable body in grubby play clothes. I'm nine. I'm not even that chubby. But I won't realize that for years.

Right now, as a child, my mother's poison seeps right into my brain without being questioned, and I start to cry. "I'm sorry."

"Sorry isn't good enough, you need to actually fix this. No more breakfast, and I want you walking back home after school from now on." My mother's face twists in a self-satisfied smirk.

The mocking expression falls off of Melody's face. "Mom, that's twenty blocks and it's mid-winter."

My mother sniffs. "The cold will make her lose weight faster."

Melody is sixteen and rail-thin, tall, blonde, perfect in my mother's eyes. But that doesn't mean she can get our mother to listen when she's on one of her rampages. "Mom, think. When she got hospitalized for double pneumonia last year the nurses called CPS. Do you want to go through that shit again?"

My mother slams a meaty palm on the table and we both jump. "Don't you swear in my house? She's walking home from now on and that's final!"

The next morning my sister slips me bus change and tells me to come home late to make it look plausible. I'm pitifully grateful, but she just scowls when I thank her. "I'm not doing it for you," she clarifies coldly. "I'm doing it to keep Mom out of jail for trying to whip your fat ass into shape."

I stare at her in astonishment and then nod as the tears fall.

I wake up with tears on my cheeks and sob aloud once before burying my face in my hands. My heart hurts; my stomach is in knots. For just a while, I was nine again—as frightened, helpless and self-loathing as ever.

I cry as quietly as possible, reminding myself that I'm okay but still weeping for the little girl I once was. I feel the soft weight of the cats and Berry curled up on me, and focus on that and other good things. The hunk downstairs flirted with me! And I think of my successes in selling my art, and that my mother is dead and can't hurt me anymore.

I'll be okay. It just hurts remembering, I ponder as my sobs and sniffles slowly dry up.

I still recall the conversation with my sister, and her snide dismissal that she was doing it because she loved me. I would steal her pocket change secretly every morning after that, and ride the bus secretly every afternoon, and our mother never found out.

And I never thanked my sister for anything ever again. And now, she's married to a man who fucks around on her, she drinks a lot, and I've left her to bitterness and misery.

I've tried to forget and even forgive, but I'm not very good at either. Sometimes, like right now, I lie awake and think about my mother, who was the size of a truck but abused her daughter for having a tummy.

Then I look up—and see a huge silhouette leaning in the doorway. I let out a startled yelp—how did he get up the stairs so quietly? Even Loki makes the stairs creak.

He moves into the room when he learns I'm awake, bare to the waist again, his skin gleaming faintly in the glow from my clock. "Are you okay?" Michael's voice is a husky whisper, thick with sleep.

"I..." I'm really not. Even reminding myself that I've long since escaped from my home town isn't working.

"I'm working on it..." I manage in a muffled voice. My hands are over my face again, glad my tears don't show in the dark.

"Holy shit, honey." He crosses the room in a few steps, concern in his voice and hands reaching for me. I freeze for a moment—and then he's sitting on the edge of the bed and his arms are around me and everything changes at once.

How long has it been since someone hugged me? Too long. I gasp, lowering my hands as my cheek makes contact with his smooth chest. My palms settle lightly over his arms.

His warmth sinks deep into me, dispelling the chill in my bones almost as fast as the agonizing loneliness. He gathers me against him.

His hand is in my hair, stroking slowly and smoothly. "It's okay," he says, and I believe him just from how his touch makes me feel.

"I have shitty dreams too," he says gently. "Does it happen to you a lot?"

"Yeah, um...not as much as it used to." The first year in Boston they happened several times a week. Then, with therapy, meds, and all the work, they started to go away. Now and again, they still come back.

And until now, there's been nothing to do about it but swallow a tranquilizer and ride it out. There's been no one to comfort me, no one to reassure me. It's so unusual I'm not sure how to respond.

He nuzzles the top of my head and I bite back a whimper.

"You all right?" I nod slightly.

"I'm...not used to being touched," I breathe.

My mother nor my sister never wanted to touch me. The only people who wanted to touch me wanted to hurt or use me. I doubt Michael wants to do either. In fact, he's going out of his way not to do the first.

"Oh." He sounds confused. "Seriously, what kind of people did you grow up around?"

I burst into tears again. It's as much from irony and relief as from pain. "They really w-were the w-worst. But aren't all people like that?"

It sounds stupid even as it comes out of my mouth, and I hide my face in his chest instead of looking at him. "Well, I honestly don't know, sweetheart, I've got no memories. But not all are. You're not. I'm not." He kisses the top of my head and I feel another rush of warmth helping me settle down again.

"That's...true..." I whisper. It's that I think everyone is terrible. But when your own mother is, when your own sister reminds you she doesn't like you, it's hard not to think everyone else must be even worse.

"Thanks for coming up," I murmur, realizing that I'm clinging to him and loosen my grip. "It helps."

"It's not a problem. I'll leave you alone now if you want," he murmurs, but I don't want that at all. All I want right now is his warmth comforting me, his heartbeat against my ear.

"I don't want you to leave me alone," I whisper in a strained voice.

I hear him suck air in surprise, and then his grip tightens on me. A shiver creeps into his breath.

"Oh," he murmurs, as I raise my head to look at him.

He brushes the tears off my cheeks with his thumb, and I gaze into his velvety black eyes. My heart is suddenly beating hard, and all words catch in my throat.

My hands are on his shoulders. His skin is so smooth that I just want to keep running my fingers over it, but I'm cautious, touching him a bit more at a time. I'm dipping in unfamiliar waters, but it feels so lovely that my nightmare memory is already fading.

I freeze when he kisses me, my hands lifting from his shoulders and fluttering in midair. The hot, sleek press of his lips teases a response out of me; I relax against him, and his hand slides up through my hair behind my braid and cradles my scalp as my head falls back.

My eyes, huge with delighted shock, stare dreamily at the ceiling as he covers my neck in kisses. Each press of his lips sends a ripple through me, like a stone tossed into a pond. And the more he does it, the more my body tingles.

He pushes aside my flannel nightie at the spot where my shoulder meets my neck, and kisses me deeply, his teeth scraping me lightly. Then he starts to suck—and I lose control and let out a low, shuddering moan.

His hand is just sliding down to cup my breast when he leans forward—and suddenly grunts in pain. "Fuck," he grumbles against my shoulder.

"Are you okay?" I gasp, some of the sexual fog going away.

"The painkiller doesn't deal with it past a certain point." He rubs my back, not lifting my head yet. "Talk about shitty timing."

"You almost died today," I try to ignore the unfamiliar defeat in my belly.

"Yeah, I just...really like you." He looks into my eyes, his expression haggard.

"I really like you too." My heart's still thumping in my ears. "And we've got at least two days together so um...maybe get more rest?"

He laughs and stretches, his shoulders popping painfully. "You're probably right."

But on his ginger way out the door, he looks back with a lopsided smile. "We'll have to take this back up tomorrow."

"Okay," I say breathlessly, and lie back, way too giddy for tears.

CHAPTER 8

Michael

G reat, now I've got a boner and a headache. Yay.

Maybe it's selfish to make a play for Eve as the reality of who I am has broken over me like a black wave. Maybe I should focus on getting my memories back before I involve her in my life?

Especially if that dream was real. Which right now, it seems to be.

Yet here I am, dick hard, lips still feeling her hesitant first kiss, lying on the sofa with my head throbbing. Maybe I shouldn't have gone upstairs?

But she was crying, and I was so sick of knowing it and giving her nothing but a few kind words. I don't know any more about putting a bullet in whoever hurt her—but I would love to put the fear of God—and me—into them.

I want an explanation for this bullshit. Why such a wonderful, woman has been made to suffer like this. My desire for justice for Eve is just as strong as my yearning to recollect. She's affected me that much.

A small thump on the stairs and then a chitter; a few seconds later Berry climbs up on the couch with me. "Hi," I murmur, as he invites himself onto the quilt and wanders onto my chest.

I hope he's had his shots.

He stares at me with his beady black eyes gleaming faintly, then chirps and wanders up to curl up under my chin. "Hey. Uh...well shit, make yourself at home then."

My chuckle jars my head again, and I grumble. When the roads open up, I better get this injury looked at. But for now, safe behind acres of snow, I'm seriously entertaining going back upstairs as soon as the pain eases up.

I wonder if ever a woman swooned against me like Eve did. That's another fogged over part. I wish to plug back into my old self, and find out where those millions are and what were my plans to get my boss off my back.

How much danger have I dragged Eve into just by collapsing on her porch? It can't be helped, but that doesn't mean I feel good about it. She needs her peace and quiet, and I don't want to screw that up.

I know not much more than she does at this point. I should tell her about the dream...but when I think about that, I tense up enough that Berry shifts uneasily and peers at me.

"Sorry, cutie." he settles back down. I should be honest with her. But I don't want to scare her in case that dream turns out to be half bullshit—or more.

Or maybe I don't want to scare her off at all?

She knows I was in a gunfight. She already suspects I could be on the wrong side of the law. She just doesn't know how bad it is.

If it is that bad, I was leaving the life anyway. And I'm rich. Somewhat.

That's when another thing about myself makes me sigh in sad exasperation...even as I smile a bit. I'm a romantic, even if I really am a killer. Already the idea of scaring Eve away has me in knots.

I lie there in the dark, with the heat from the pellet stove lapping against me, trying to remember more until I finally drop off to sleep.

I wake up disoriented but rested, tiny raccoon paws playing with my lower lip. "Hey, stop, that's my face." I gently push him away and he starts playing with my fingers instead. I open an eye and see light coming down the stairs; Eve turned everything off down here.

What time is it? I scoop Berry into one arm and sit up carefully, wary of my head. It feels better, however the surface wound is starting to itch. It probably needs to be washed again.

I go into the bathroom with Berry trailing behind and take another shower, wishing for a change of clothes. I'll be wearing these jeans for a couple of days, seems like. But by the time I'm clean, dried and dressed again, I feel a lot better.

When I come out, Eve is at the window, corner of the window quilt peeled aside. She has changed to paint-spattered jeans and an outsized purple turtleneck. I make some noise, and she looks back, offering me a small, tight smile.

"Good morning." I stand behind her, sliding a hand over her shoulder as I peer outside. "...oh. Well shit."

Still white-out conditions, and enough snow piled up on the porch it'll need a lot of shoveling. I huff out a sigh. "I'll help you the storm blows over."

"Thanks, but um...how are you feeling?" She refastens the quilt and turns to me, worry in her eyes.

"Better. Getting some sleep helped, though neither of us got much." I slide my hand up the back of her neck and her eyes hood; when I kiss her, she responds less hesitantly, cupping my jawline with her hand. Her mouth tastes of mouthwash; she must have gotten up recently.

"That's good," she utters when the kiss breaks.

I cuddle her close, her full breasts cozy against my chest and her heart beating fast in spite of her gentle smile. "So, can you show me your paintings?"

"Breakfast first," she declares and I nod.

"Do you have coffee?" The craving's creeping up on me almost as fast as the yearning for the sex I can't have yet.

"Yeah, I can't drink it often but I keep it for baking." I let her go and she moves away half-heartedly before going to the kitchen.

Two cats and a raccoon are lined up at their food bowls. Berry's has a variety of fruits, nuts and some cat food, along with a small bowl of water. As I look their way Berry has a blueberry in his hands and is carefully washing it.

Eve putters around putting the kettle on and setting up the coffee filter over a mug, then brings another bowl of chopped fruit, nuts and seeds out for Diogenes. I settle at the table, listening to them chat as the kettle heats.

"Hey little man. Let's change your sweater before you eat." Rustling, the rattle of seeds in the bowl as she puts it in its holder.

"Mango!" screeches the bird.

"Yes, there's some mango. Here's your red sweater. No, the sweater first." More rustling. "Good boy! Here you go. Now I'll just change your lining."

She comes back crumpling up a newspaper and shoves it into a bin under the sink. "I'll be right with you, just doing my morning stuff."

"No problem. You want some help with anything?" I could really get used to this. It's boring but part of that is just being snowed in.

And right now, it's a haven away from a world I'm not ready to deal with yet. A haven that I get to share with her. And that's enough.

CHAPTER 9

Carolyn

"The good news is there's no sign of problems at the lodge," I say into my phone as I watch Lucca's youngest son at the other end of the bar. He's drinking heavily with at least four bodyguards. Two huge guys flanking him, two being not-so-inconspicuous at a nearby table.

They haven't noticed me, which makes me ashamed for them.

"No sign of Di Lorenzo?" Daniels sounds annoyed. He suspects he's sent me in the wrong direction. I do too. The problem is, we know where he'll lay the blame in his report to his superior.

"Nobody even remotely close to his description. I have a guy on the security cameras twenty-four-seven and lodge security is cooperating."

"No chance of someone sneaking in from outside? Things are dead in Boston. Nobody's made a play for the older brother, and the middle one is in protective custody." He's grumbling, and the fact that nothing's going on in Boston makes my heart sink.

"Sir, we're cut off up here. Whiteout conditions with winds up to forty miles an hour and an increasing avalanche risk. If Di Lorenzo isn't in place he won't get to us for at least another couple of days." If he's coming up here at all.

A creeping worry that either he was never coming to the Berkshires, or Prometheus is right and hitters from the Sixth Family got to him first. That second alternative bothers me. I need a win, something to get Daniels off my back.

The idea of the Sixth Family gunning down another suspect has me clutching my bottom-shelf rum and Coke white-knuckled.

"So you're going to just hang out on the Bureau's dime?" His voice is so snide that I set down my glass with a hard clack.

"My coming up here was your call, sir. I'm maintaining surveillance on the potential target." My voice has no tone to it.

"No need to get angry," he mocks...and then when I don't respond with an outburst, there's a disappointed silence.

Daniels, you are a fucking child, and I'll be there when your bullshit finally comes back to bite you. "Anything else, sir?" I ask in that same toneless voice.

"No, not much to do until the weather clears. Maintain surveillance and see if there's anything you can dig up on Di Lorenzo. You've probably missed something."

"Yes sir." He hangs up, and I put the phone away before downing the rest of my drink and muttering, "Prick."

How have I managed to get up here before the storm hit? The sky got blacker and lower with every mile I made it up the highway. And the whole time, I was wondering if it was the right thing to come here.

Daniels's direction isn't very good for an Assistant Director. But as long as he has subordinates to take the fall, his job is secure. Mine...depends on impressing him.

I'm getting sick of it.

Lucca is getting drunker, and eventually his men join in. Is he mourning his father's murder, or celebrating it?

I would be celebrating. And Lucca's daughter Melissa probably is, right this second.

Something was very sad that the best thing I could do in the case of Lucca's fleeting daughter was help her make a clean getaway with Chase. It meant to let Chase go, except for the problems it caused my career, I don't care about that.

Besides helping me catch Lucca, Alan Chase never killed anybody, unlike Michael Di Lorenzo. And yet now I'm almost worried about that darn assassin. Am I too sentimental for this work?

I'm sipping the water off my ice when the bartender brings me a hot buttered rum and a slice of chocolate raspberry torte from the restaurant. "Um, hi, thanks, but I didn't order this," I say, confused, as he sets it in front of me."

"Table in the corner ordered it," the burly guy flashes a smile at me and goes back to polishing glasses.

I look over—and the table's deserted. A sealed envelope on top with my name in a beautiful handwritten script. A quick look around —but whoever it is has disappeared. I retrieve the envelope and return to my chair, wondering.

I take a sip of the drink: top shelf liquor, as luxuriant on the tongue as the torte. My "admirer" has spared no expense. Lucca?

His men are carrying him back to his room as they laugh and joke about it. No, he's in no shape for something this subtle.

I open the envelope and pull out a single sheet of typed paper.

Sorry for the intrusion, Special Agent, but in the absence of other reliable sources, I thought you would like an update on Mr. Di Lorenzo. He has survived the attempt on his life and has taken shelter in the mountains. His former employers know he is alive and will search for him.

I am not in the lodge. I used a messenger. Do not waste time searching for me. When the storm is over, go to these GPS coordinates to find Di Lorenzo's car and other important evidence.

I cannot give you Di Lorenzo, Carolyn, as much as I would like to. He is needed. But the men after him have committed acts of violence on American soil with strong evidence against them and will be much easier to make a case.

Get some rest. You never sleep enough.

It isn't signed. It doesn't have to be. It's Prometheus.

"Damn," I mutter. "At least one reliable source. Too bad he's borderline creepy and probably a criminal himself." And for some reason, he doesn't want me bringing Di Lorenzo in. Well, he's going to live with disappointment in this case.

I note down the GPS coordinates; they correspond with a stretch of highway maybe five miles off. If Prometheus's letter is correct, Di Lorenzo is just as stuck in the area as the rest of us. Which means I still have a chance.

I wonder, though, why he is bargaining for the man. Is Prometheus with the Sixth Family? No, that doesn't make sense, unless he's deliberately sacrificing the hitters he's offering in Di Lorenzo's place.

Why is he needed? Why am I being urged not to let another of my assigned suspects go?

He's right about one thing, though. If I can grab some of Di Lorenzo's "coworkers" it should satisfy Daniels no matter what.

Why would Prometheus need a hitter if the guy's trying to get out of the business?

So many questions. And the man who can answer them is somewhere else, safely behind a phone and a computer screen while unknown numbers of men carry out his orders.

I finish the drink and dessert, and go upstairs to get some sleep. Whoever I bring in depends on who I find first.

I just know one thing: I'm not coming out of these mountains empty-handed.

CHAPTER 10

Eve

The day passes too quickly, despite the storm. Michael saw my talents. We played with my pets and made lunch. He continues to recover. And he remembers more.

"Someone stepped in front of my car and shot at me. I don't remember the crash." He's drinking his coffee as we watch the sunset through the remnants of the storm. The temperature's rising enough that I can keep the window quilt off for a while.

"Do you know why?" His arm is around me. It feels so good that I want to stay quiet, and not talk about anything. But we still have a puzzle to solve.

I just...don't want to solve it too quickly. I want him to stay here. It's totally selfish and illogical, and I should know better than to hang on to him too tightly, but...

I'm falling for him. That's never happened before, and I just...can't stand being abandoned again.

But I know he'll leave. Something dangerous is waiting for him out there, a life I have no clue about. The life he's forgotten involves shootings and car crashes, and even the name he's remembered might not be his.

What am I getting into? It's so ironic that this potentially perilous man is the first to like me, and the first to be kind.

I should prepare myself to let him go. I should just get used to the idea that he's going to walk away, and at this rate, he'll be taking my heart with him. His liking and desiring me may not be enough for him to stay,

He's looking at me quietly, as if trying to figure out what to say. "I don't know yet. I dreamed about it, but I don't know how much of it was real.

"Once we dig out from the storm tomorrow morning, I'm going to go down on the road and see if anything I recollect about that crash was real." His hand gently kneads my shoulder. "I'll know then whether what I saw in my dream was real or not."

I nod, ignoring the huge lump in my throat. "I'll miss you when you go," I admit as I turn to him.

In response, he takes me in his arms and kisses me. It's very gentle this time, and lingers, until I'm breathless and trembling against him. My thighs squeeze together and my knees are going to buckle.

The kiss breaks. "I'll miss you too," he breathes against my lips. Then he winces, and pushes himself back as if forcing himself. "Anyway, you can invite me back."

I blink, surprised that hadn't even occurred to me. I just figured when he walked out of my life, he would do it for good. "You...would come back?"

He gives me a gently pained look. "Of course I would. You saved my life and looked after me when you had no reason to. I know almost nothing of my past, but people as good as you are uncommon."

"Oh." I didn't know whether to be reassured or disappointed. "I hope you don't feel like you owe me something."

He chuckles and shakes his head. "Of course I do. But that's not why I'll come back."

That reassures me more than his gratitude, but now I'm confused. "Then...why will you?"

Another kiss—and this one becomes deep and fierce, leaving me swooning in his arms. "I'll show you later," he promises with a mischievous smile.

That's enough to leave me floating around on a cloud for a solid hour before my doubts wear away my bliss. I've never had sex before, and the only things keeping him off me are his head and my anxiety. I have to find a way to calm down that won't knock me out like the sleeping pills.

"Michael," I ask as he's making a couple of chicken breasts with capers, "What was your nightmare about?"

He looks at me peculiarly, and then looks down. "I barely remember. I got into an argument with someone. I think he was a close friend. And maybe twenty minutes later I was ambushed."

"So...you think whoever your friend was set you up?" I try not to sound worried.

"I'm not sure. Maybe. Not much in that dream made sense." He busies himself with flipping the filets. "Only my name really feels familiar. That and the ambush itself."

"So you're...going to find the spot where you crashed?" There's something he's not telling me. I'm usually the one who is bad at eye contact, but right now, it's his eyes that are looking everywhere but at me.

"Yeah, that's the plan." He hesitates, then looks at me. "How long does it take them to plow out the roads here again?"

"We're usually clear by mid-afternoon." I check outside; it's dark now and the moon is out, making all that snow glow blue-white. No sign of a bird or beast. I'll need to throw out some fodder tomorrow morning.

Hopefully the bears are properly asleep by now, despite the mild winter we've had.

"How's it looking?" He leans away from the stove to peer outside. "Besides beautiful."

"Six foot drifts in places. We're doing okay here but I'm not getting the Jeep out of the garage without a lot of digging." It'll be a lot easier with help, at least.

"That won't be a problem." He transfers the chicken breasts onto plates and squeezes some lime juice into the pan, mixing it all together. "Too bad you don't have any cooking wine."

"Sorry about that. I don't keep alcohol in the house. Reacts badly with my meds. And too many drinkers in my family already." I'm slightly embarrassed to admit my caution around alcohol, but he just smiles.

"It's fine, I only drink sometimes, and today it seems like a bad idea anyway with my head." He looks thoughtful as he works. "Hey Eve...ask you something?"

I look up from setting the table. "What is it?"

"You don't seem much freaked out that I got shot at. I might not be all that great a person, you know." And he's not looking at me anymore again.

I take a deep breath to steady myself before I answer. "Michael...my life has been full of things that most people would be traumatized with. It's left me petrified of every human, not just the bad ones. I have to spend a lot of time pretending not to be afraid when...when I'm scared of people, especially in groups.

"If you're some kind of criminal and you find that out, just don't bring it to my door. I don't want any trouble in my life, I came here to get away from people's bad treatment of each other."

He looks back up at me again. "But?"

"But...I know what bad persons are like. You...whatever you've had to do to survive, that's your business. I'm mostly worried about you— not that you're going to hurt me. Except...maybe by leaving." I can't keep my sadness out of my tone.

"Maybe I'll be lucky and it turns out that I'm James Bond or something?" He means his joke to be reassuring, but I've read the Ian Fleming books.

"James Bond was a government-sanctioned professional killer," I point out—and he drops the tongs he's using into the pan. "What is it?" his look is haunted. "Are you recalling something else?"

"Maybe," he rasps distractedly. "I'm not quite sure yet. But you're right about one thing, honey. I would never willingly hurt you."

My eyes are stinging suddenly. "Well...that's almost a first in my life. So...thank you."

He grins wryly. "No problem. You make it easy to care about you, Eve."

CHAPTER 11

Eve

I take half a tranquilizer after supper, knowing I need to relax. Michael and I curl up on the couch and watch an adventure movie on my laptop, each of us with a cat on our laps. The movie excites Diogenes, who comments obscenely and once gets into a mock-argument with Michael.

Berry is wandering. Now and again I have to set Freya aside and pull him out of a cabinet or off a light fixture. Outside, the temperature keeps dropping; the heater struggles to maintain the room at sixty five degrees despite our constant refilling of the pellet stove.

Michael and I hold hands a lot. He's taking the painkillers, and they still aren't strong enough. I see him wincing now and again, and feel a mix of concern and distress that he's still in pain.

"How are you feeling?" I ask once the movie's over.

"I need another round of ibuprofen and maybe a nap." He sees the disappointment on my face and flashes a grin. "I owe you a rain check for something. Can we postpone for a few more hours?"

"I'll try to find the time," I tease as he leans over to kiss me.

Damn, I think as I lie awake staring at the ceiling. That delicious giddiness still bubbles inside of me, keeping me from being too disappointed. But my body is full of cravings I tried to forget about for years—cravings that have never been satisfied.

It's okay. We have time, and we both want it. It will be all right.

I'm warm under all my covers, but the bedroom is chilly; even with the cover taken off the metal stovepipe that runs through the center of the room, the cool air makes my cheeks sting. Michael has promised to refill the pellets in the stove tonight, so at least I don't have to jump out of my cozy bed to deal with it in the middle of the night.

I doze off, with no dreams to wake me up in tears this time. Just a creeping disenchantment that can't go away—at least, until I'm in Michael's arms again.

Fortunately, that won't be long.

A faint creak on the stairs. All the animals but Loki are downstairs, where it's warmer. . I look up--and see Michael standing in the doorway, his face in shadow.

"Hey, you okay?" I ask softly as he crosses to me.

He's quiet for a moment, then reaches down and slides his hand slowly through my hair, wrapping his fingers briefly around the base of my braid. "I'm fine."

"You sure?" My heart starts beating faster; he promised me something as soon as he felt better. That takes me to an unfamiliar territory.

"Mind if I join you?" he purrs, and for a few moments the words catch in my throat and I stay quiet or risk letting out an embarrassing squeak.

"Um, okay!" Oh God, that sounded terrible!

He chuckles softly and sits on the edge of my bed, taking me into his arms. "Feeling nervous? Is there any way I can reassure you?"

Oh boy. "Um...do you have any condoms in that wallet?" I'm really not used to this.

"Oh, that." He slides a hand into his pant pocket and deposits three of them on my nightstand. "They were in my pants. I guess you didn't search me there."

"Um, no, that seemed a little..." Awkward! Like now, but without the warmth, or his invitation to touch. Which I'm still working up the nerve to do.

He strokes his hand down my back, leaving a tingling trail behind, and I shiver and tilt my head, offering my mouth as he takes me in his arms again.

There were so many ways to kiss! Soft, tentative, confident, fierce, tender, teasing, sensual, delicate... We go through them all, the intensity between us swelling and ebbing in waves until I'm gasping for air between kisses.

When he finally leans back, I'm breathless and wet, the tops of my thighs already slick with my juices. He's feeling it too: tremors run through his muscles as I run my fingertips over his back.

"I never knew it could be like this," I gasp softly as he cuddles me.

He flashes a grin. "We're lucky I've still got my skills. Don't remember where I learned them, but you can still enjoy them."

I realize then what he means: everything is new to him too. When I stroke his back, he trembles because he has no memory of what that feels like--any more than I do! His hands know what to do, but he has no more memory of experiencing such pleasures.

Does he know what an orgasm feels like? Am I even capable myself?

But then again, most men wouldn't even interest me. I started to wonder whether all those years of hiding my desires to keep myself safe from more bullying had killed the flame in me forever. Now I know that's not true. Maybe none of my doubts about sex and my body are true--not with the right man, anyway.

And this is positively the right man.

He moves away from me and stands. He is unbuttoning his jeans. "I'll just get rid of these now."

My eyes widening as the zipper rasps down and he slowly pushes the denim off his hips. His short pubic hairs gleam slightly in the light from downstairs...and then he shucks his trousers completely, taking his boxers with them.

His cock springs up against his belly and I tense, slightly intimidated by its size. I've never been up close and personal with a penis before, and his is almost as big around as my wrist. I immediately feel my pussy clench in both desire and tension. How can I possibly fit him inside me without pain?

He grins when he sees me staring. "Do you like what you see?"

"Yes," I breathe. "But...how could that even fit inside of me?"

He reaches for one of the condoms and rolls it on. "By getting you nice and wet and relaxed first."

His grin fades, and he reaches for the edge of the covers. "Can I come in? I'm actually freezing."

I giggle and scoot over and he slides in next to me. I let out an eep as his cold feet slide against my leg. "Eek! Cold!"

He laughs. "Sorry, sweetheart. I promise to warm you up."

Loki gets jostled one time too many and springs off the bed with some kitty grumbling. "Sorry, furball, but I don't do threesomes," Michael jokes, and I blush down to my toes.

He turns and kisses me deeply, hands starting to slide over my body through my nightgown. He explores every inch of me, from my knees to the top of my head, like a blind man mapping the contours of my body. His smooth hands tease and stroke me through the cloth, and I shiver and tentatively begin exploring his body too.

His skin is so suave; even his scars feel like oil-rubbed leather, barely raised.

I lose track of time as we trace each other's skin with our hands. Then he finds the bottom of my nightgown with his fingertips and slides his hand under it, caressing my thigh.

I moan softly. "More," I sigh, and he smiles and starts tugging the gown up my body.

Every inch that the flannel slides up, the more caresses he lavishes on my skin. His nimble fingers unbutton the gown's bodice so he can press kisses into my neck, his mouth wandering downward into my cleavage.

His thumb digs into the crease of my hip and sends unexpected pleasure shooting through my pussy, just as strongly as if he caressed me directly.

When he lifts the gown past my belly, I get impatient and sit up enough to pull it off. He stares as my breasts lift close to his face, and then follows me back down to the mattress, reaching to cradle them like treasures.

He kneels over me, thumbs flicking at my nipples as I squirm and lift my hips reflexively.

"There we go," he rasps softly. "Do you like that?"

"Oh yes," I moan, already panting for breath. "Please don't stop..."

"I can't," he murmurs, lowering his head to my breasts.

He starts kissing them, running his tongue over them, nibbling lightly. Then his tongue starts circling the edge of my areola, and I tense slightly, not knowing what to anticipate.

His hot mouth closes over my nipple and he sucks delicately, and my mind fogs over with delight.

He has full control; every long pull of his mouth brings me up on my heels and the back of my head as if my body's suspended by ropes. His mouth works against my flesh, tugging and licking, while electric shocks of pleasure leave me trembling and clinging to him.

I whimper in disappointment when he finishes suckling my breasts and starts kissing my belly under the covers instead. His fingertips trace over my skin, the small push of my tummy; his tongue trails downward and darts into my navel.

I'm so turned on now that I can barely think. All I can do is writhe and make noises as he moves lower and lower, until he's looping one of my legs over his shoulder and leaning in to breathe warm air over my aching, tingling pussy.

I'm realizing what he's about to do when he strokes the lips of my pussy open with his fingertips, and then slides them into me slowly as he leans forward to taste me.

"Oh!" The dart of his tongue, the way it slides up and down and then starts circling and fluttering against my clit, excites me so much that my muscles tighten almost painfully.

He has to pin me down; every stroke of his tongue has me whimpering and rolling my hips. I dig my nails into the bedding on either side of me and my heel into the quilt as his tongue lashes against my pussy again and again.

A delicious pressure building inside of me, it's scary, but mostly it feels so good that all I can do is beg half-coherently for more. Then, his two fingers inside of me start stroking my walls, and suddenly the pressure builds so high that I'm sobbing for air.

Pleasure becomes ecstasy moments later, every cell in me lights up from my clit outward. My burning desire expands to engulf me; I scream with sheer joy.

And he just keeps going.

Unbelievable! After that frenzy my body doesn't rest; he starts suckling my clit delicately, and another climax roars through me instantly. This time, I don't have the breath to scream; I moan hoarsely instead.

Finally, he raises up from me; I flop to the mattress, almost completely limp. He climbs over me, breathing hard; when his head emerges from the blankets, his eyes burn with yearn.

I take him into my arms, thighs already parted. My relaxed pussy feels the push of his cock head, and then he's sliding into me, stretching me open enjoyably. It barely hurts!

His head falls back and he groans, eyes wide. "Oh God," he gasps, and presses in deeper, his whole body trembling. "You feel so fucking good..."

The smell of my juices are mixing with his sweat and the musk of his arousal as he starts to thrust slowly. His breathing stutters; he speeds gradually, the mattress springs starting to creak under us.

I hold him, hips lifting to meet his as I start to get turned on again. His hot shaft sinks into me gently over and over, rubbing me in places no one has touched, making my clit tingle all over again.

Harder and faster he moves, and it feels incredible. No pain, no awkwardness, no detachment from the moment or my body; when my nails rake his back he just groans with pleasure and thrusts harder.

I feel him going rigid as he moves and his breath is more erratic; he starts to groan in time with his thrusts, each one louder and more full-throated than the next. The bed's shaking; I'm shaking.

I try to whisper encouragement but only manage incoherent coos as he pounds into me. His cries get more desperate...and then I hear mine rise to join his as my cunt contracts around him again.

My orgasm touches his off; even as I moan and writhe under him, his back arches and he shouts with pure bliss.

His cock spasms inside of me; he is stretched above me, face transformed by ecstasy. Then he shudders a last time, and settles over me.

"Oh, Michael," I croon with the last of my strength. He drags himself up and kisses me softly.

"Did you like that?" he murmurs drowsily, a lazy smile on his lips.

"Yes," I coo, shocked and gratified. "Oh, yes."

"Good." He gets off of me reluctantly and slips out from under the covers to get rid of the condom. "Because once we get some rest, I want more."

I smile, barely able to keep my eyes open. "Me too."

CHAPTER 12

Michael

I wake up in Eve's bed and wonder if I've done the wrong thing. If that dream really is right, I've already dragged her into a chaos she may never forgive me for. And yet she made it clear she'll accept me no matter who I am.

That got me all choked up! What was my life like outside of the incidents in my head from the dream? But never have I felt such unconditional acceptance.

Maybe I've been spending too much time around shitty people myself?

I roll over to watch Eve sleep. She's naked under the covers, her bare skin silky against mine. My cock goes from its morning half-staff to fully erect in seconds as I breathe in her scent.

She stirs and opens her eyes, murmuring sleepily. "Good morning," I purr, and she smiles as I press close to her.

"Good morning."

I kiss her delicately, one hand sliding up to cup her full breast.

Her nipple tightens into a point as I run my thumb over it, she squirms and lets out a soft whimper against my lips. I clamber over her, bracing most of my weight on my knees as I keep the kiss going.

I take the head of my cock and prop it against her clit, rubbing it up and down as she starts to shiver and lifts her hips under me. Her hands go over my hips and cup my ass, then caress my back as she pulls me closer. Her sighs and gasps turn into a muffled moan and she digs her fingertips lightly against my skin.

Her slick flesh against the head of my cock hardens me further, the jolts of pleasure sending shivers through me. I hold out, teasing and cuddling her, resisting the urge to thrust into her and pound away until I release. The methods of sex might still be in my hands and body, but the pleasures of sex are delightfully novel.

Lastly the kiss breaks and I bury my face in her neck, nibbling and licking at her pulse and then sucking when she starts to rock her hips harder against me. I'm breathing heavily now, cock aching with the need for her...and when she cups my ass roughly, nails digging against my skin, I know she's ready.

I roll on one of the remaining condoms, then replace my cock with two fingers and stroke her as I enter. She arches her back, lips parting with inclination. Her eyes are squeezed closed.

Nothing feels as good as the hot, clinging walls of her pussy taking me in, even with the condom. I stiffen, gasping for air as I enter inch by tender inch. Then, patiently, I lie over her, propped up on one hand and thrust in deep, holding still as I keep teasing at her clit.

Her head falls back on the pillow; her muscles tighten, and her flesh clenches closer around me until I'm fighting the urge to thrust. I want it so badly...but wait, working my fingers steadily, until she starts to thrash.

The contractions make her scream again, howling with desire, grinding and arching against me as she milks my shaft. I groan through my teeth and thrust rapidly, our bellies smacking together as I flick my fingertips against her clit faster and faster.

She squeals; her nails dig in enough to sting—and then she's clenching around me again, moaning hoarsely as I pound into her. This time, her wild response drags me over the edge; I go rigid, back arching, waves of ecstasy breaking over me. I groan at the ceiling as my cock spills endless gouts of sperm.

Everything whites out for a few moments; when I come to, I'm settling my head on her shoulder, and she's holding me as we catch our breaths.

Only when I feel my erection start to dwindle do I force myself up to get rid of the condom. The cold air slaps my bare skin; I add a few pellets to the stove on my way back from the bathroom. Then back upstairs to Eve's bed, and her arms.

Relaxed, satisfied, I close my eyes, glad to have the lunacy of my situation outside her front door for a while.

It doesn't last, though. I haven't even finished my shower before worrying about my dream, Bertie and the strong possibility that I'm a mob killer on the run.

I'm still preoccupied as we dig out the porch and then the car hours later. I don't want to leave Eve behind, but unless Bertie and his associates lose my track they may be coming after me incessantly. And her home is walking distance from wherever I crashed. Who knows whether they have a team out scouring the woods for me?

A snow blower makes quick work of the snow, which hasn't had a chance to get icy yet. And the Jeep has a small plow on the front for the driveway. I sit in the passenger seat and chat with Eve as she drives back and forth clearing the path to the highway.

"So, the bad news is that the urgent care center's not open. We can go to the hospital twenty miles further, or wait until tomorrow." She utters an exasperated sigh. "Did I mention that I hate snowstorms?"

"I can certainly sympathize, though in this case the storm gave us time to know each other better." Especially carnally.

The way she screamed with shocked pleasure when she had her first orgasm... How she thrashed under me, hips pumping, pussy contracting around me until I gave in and she drained every drop from my shuddering cock.

I can't wait to find the car, prove that it exists, and grab anything that might help from it. Not just because it will help me piece together my past, but because afterward, we can go home and ravage each other again.

After that, though, I have to figure out what to do about my pursuers, and let Eve know the ugly truth. How am I going to do that?

The road is covered with a thin layer of salty slush when we break through the berm the snowplows left and drive onto it. Only a few sets of tire tracks crossing it; almost no one came out today, not even to ski. "Nasty out here," I comment. "Kind of surprised the power didn't go out."

"I have a backup generator, we would have been fine. That becomes a problem when the wind kicks up, and the trees cut it a lot. Last time the power went out was because lightning hit a trans-former." She slows down as a squirrel scrambles across the road.

"At least the wildlife is out," I comment as it goes away.

"Yeah," she breathes wistfully. "Two days without being out and around and they'll take the opportunity to get some sun and forage the first chance they have."

"You really like animals a lot, don't you?" I think it's adorable.

"Yeah, I really do. They're more honorable than most humans." Her smile gets strained for a moment, but she simply drives on.

We don't pass cars on our way down the road. I look around for some familiar landmark. Then we pass a tree split by lightning- and remember it from my dream.

"We're going the right direction. Continue this way." My body is tensing as we make our way toward the site where I was ambushed.

"Are you recalling more?" She sounds expectant, but something is looming I don't want to evoke.

It comes anyway; suddenly my hands are on the wheel of a larger car, driving faster, the road clear and the slope above me barely crusted with snow. Anger and grief, my sense of betrayal, my worry— and yes, my fear, though I'm not letting it stop me. I've never been that kind of person.

I can't believe this! Bertie, my cousin, my only living family. I helped him immigrate and get his job with the Don.

And what does he do to repay me when I tell him I can't do this shit anymore? What does he decide is the appropriate response to his kin and best friend refusing to execute a kid?

He points a gun at me and tries to force me. That son-of-a-bitch should have known better!

Fine, forget it. I'm passing the ski lodge and continuing west until I hit the state line. Then just keep going southwest. Colorado sounds good.

I come out of it blinking and sucking air. "Are you all right?" Eve asks, all tender concern.

"I had some kind of dust-up with an old friend and coworker. Not sure what he wanted me to do, but I knocked him out and left him behind. Then I drove down this road." A lot of details are out. It's cowardly, but I don't want to scare her off.

Do I get to keep her if she finds out about my old job? So all mention of it sticks in my throat.

"So you do think that your friend set you up?" She sounds bothered, not repulsed. Do I even deserve this loyalty and support?

Well, I'll do whatever I can to earn it. Now that I'm realizing how incredibly rare it is to find someone this loving. How unusual it is to find someone worth letting my guard down around.

If I can keep her, and make her happy, maybe I can start again as a good man, and not a killer. But anyone after me should be off my back first.

"I'm quite certain. Not quite sure why." I feel terrible about holding out on her. But she doesn't need to be afraid of me, and if she finds out I used to be a hitter for the Montreal mob, she might be.

"So you said it was about ten minutes down the road?" she slows down. "Let's look for a break in the guardrail."

"Good idea." It will have to be there— once we find the car, I'll have even more pieces of this riddle.

Including, hopefully, an idea of how to get away from the people after me. Right now, my only real hope is that they think I'm already dead.

"That's it up ahead," A work crew is on the road. "They're

repairing the break. We'll have to park at the next turnoff and hike."
My heart sinks at the fact that the crash site is tangible, but I was
bracing myself for this.

"I'm game," she answers instantly. "I need to stretch my legs after
all that time indoors." She has no idea that it looks like what I'm
about to prove—my story—is even creepier than we suspected.

We pass the construction site; five guys in vests repairing the
barrier, and two more standing around drinking coffee. A blue sedan
is parked near the construction equipment.

One of the guys takes a long look at me as we drive past. He
doesn't look familiar, but that doesn't comfort me.

We park at the nearest turn-off and I help Eve over the barrier
and down into the woods below the road. Snow is piled everywhere,
of course, but fortunately, a lot more level than the road above. Away
from the barrier, under the shelter of the pines, it's walkable.

I'm carrying a shovel, she has her portable snow blower and an
extra battery pack. We also have a couple of empty backpacks. The
rental is certainly not in shape to drive out of here; I'm not even vexed
about returning it. But anything of mine could be evidence, and I
need to get it out of there before anyone notices the car and gets
curious.

We hold hands as we walk. I can't feel her warmth through the
gloves; I'm just glad that I can help her along. We intentionally stay
out of sight of the work crew as we cut around toward the crash site
from below.

What are we going to find? Some of my personal belongings must
be in there. What will happen if getting them back brings another
flood of ugly memories, ones I might not want to share with Eve?

But I'll have to. Once we get back, we´ll sit down and discuss
everything that I've managed to confirm so far. It may scare her off,
but it's still my obligation.

"Why nobody has come to drag the car out of here?" Eve inquires
as we draw within view of the break in the barrier. We're just down-
hill from it now, and I peer around among the mounds of snow,
looking for an indication of my rental.

"Maybe they couldn't see it? I'm having trouble finding it myself." I shade my eyes from the unexpected glare of the sun, which sparkles off the snow like a field of diamonds. Only the blue shadows under the pines provide relief from the blinding view; I try to focus on them.

Branches are broken off the trees and the brush is torn up from the repair site to a big mound of snow down the slope from us. I let out a sigh of relief. "There we go. C'mon."

Up the slope, the tops of orange helmets are visible as the men work on bolting sections of fresh barrier into place. "Okay. We need to dig out one of the doors and the trunk without drawing attention. Let's avoid using the blower unless I get worn out."

She nods, and we walk over to the buried car and get to work. Fortunately, the snow hasn't crusted over yet; the mound is in shadow and it's not warm enough. I dig out powder in a straight line until I find a corner of the red car, and then excavate until I find the trunk. "Okay, here's part of it."

I fish out my keys and try every one until one fits and turns. The lid pops open, the remainder of the snow sliding off of it, and a single hard-sided gray suitcase is inside.

"Okay, here we go." I pull it out and then move around to what I'm hoping is the passenger side door. "I'll have to lug my suitcase back up to the road. It's pretty heavy. Can you handle the shovel as well as the blower on the way back?"

She nods in determination. "Absolutely." She's excited to find out who I am as well.

I hope she's not disappointed!

The passenger side door opens after a lot of shoveling, scraping and tugging that leaves me overheated enough to take off my hat for a bit. Then I clamber inside.

The windshield is shattered, snow all over the front seat. More digging. A few drops of blood dried in the pale blue upholstery. That ambush played up exactly as I dredge up. Even the bullet hole that has gone through the dashboard.

"Yeah, that part of the dream was definitely right," I sigh.

"Getting cold?" she asks, and I look up to see her holding out a big silver Thermos.

"Oh wow, honey, is that where the rest of this morning's pot of coffee went? You're a Godsend." She really is! Coffee, kindness, great sex and she adores me! "I am so fortunate to have met you."

She blushes adorably. "I um, doctored it with some chocolate," she admits. "It makes it more palatable."

"Field mocha? Okay." I unscrew the top and take a swallow, stinging my tongue but sending welcome warmth all through me. "This is good."

I take a few minutes' break to rest and warm up with the coffee. We trade the Thermos back and forth and drink from it until it's gone; I drink most of it. Digging out a car from a snowdrift is tough work. I brace myself and get back to it as soon as the Thermos is dry.

In the glove box, a stack of cash I shoved into a pocket, rental documents, and a pair of heated gloves. In the foot wells, a lot of broken glass, a shattered pair of driving glasses, and a .44 automatic I hastily slip into the empty holster under my arm before Eve can see it. I immediately feel more secure with a gun on my person.

It's probably from a habit so old that it's changed my emotions. I'll have hide the piece from Eve until I can explain it without freaking her out. Maybe in the suitcase once I've emptied it out?

As a final point, under the brake pedal, I find something unexpected: another cellphone, saved from the snow completely by chance in an air pocket under the pedal. I recognize it at once. "Hey, I just found my phone."

"The other one isn't yours?" She peeks in the door at it.

"Yeah, that might be why I couldn't remember it's unlock code." I swipe experimentally, but of course, the battery's dead. "I hope the charger's in my suitcase."

"Would make sense if you didn't find it in your clothes," she speculates.

The back seat is clear of both snow and any items that might be personal. "Okay," I breathe, relieved that none of the construction workers have overheard us talking over the noise of their work. "I think we're done here."

"Good, because I'm freezing my toes off. Do you want to head into town for anything, or go home?" Her voice is cheery despite her mild complaint.

Thinking about her cabin in the woods, warm and snug and full of endearing critters, and the big quilt-piled bed where she held me in the dark. My cock starts to firm up despite the cold, and I smile. "Yeah, I want a chance to go through my stuff someplace warm and private."

I'm grabbing the suitcase and getting ready to follow Eve up the trail we broke when I hear a female shout from the construction site. I look up—and see a woman with a white braid picking her way down the slope toward us.

"Hey!" she's yelling. "FBI! Empty your hands and stop where you are!"

"What—" Eve starts, but I simply shake my head.

"Drop the gear and run for it," I tell her—and she does, dropping the shovel and snow blower and stumbling up the hill as fast as she can. Thank God. I book it after her.

"Michael Di Lorenzo! Stop or I'll shoot!" comes the yell, and I duck, running after Eve with the suitcase slung over my back.

"What's going on?" Eve gasps in alarm as she runs ahead of me, making good time despite her small, round build.

"That woman is not FBI," I rasp in response. Some men are yelling up on the road now. Eve whimpers in fright and pushes to run faster. "Or if she is, she's fucking crazy!"

"I'm starting to believe you!" Eve tosses over her shoulder. I hear the woman cursing, and then she shouts once and the yelling stops.

"We have to hurry. She'll have guessed that we parked down the road." I push ahead and grab Eve's hand with my free one, helping her along as we rush back to her Jeep.

"Who is she?" Eve puffs, sounding flustered.

"I don't know, but I don't trust her not to put a bullet in us if she catches up." Even if she is FBI, I can't expect that she won't shoot.

Fucking Bureau agents! Just what I need: two different trigger-happy groups coming after me. Though if she really is FBI, there may be a way to get her chasing Bertie and his backup instead?

How did they know to set me up when I had Bertie's phone the whole time? They must have already been in the area—which meant either the Family sent them as my backup—or as his, if I refused their "side job".

Was my loyalty questionable? Was I showing signs of wanting to leave? Or did they want rid of me knowing I would never murder a child, even on their say-so?

All these questions gnaw at me as we stumble our way back to the Jeep. I'm still praying that somehow, that woman picked her way down the slope and follow us directly. Otherwise, all she has to do is get in that blue sedan, drive down a bit, and—

And when we get there, it's exactly as I feared. The blue sedan is parked close behind us, and the blonde woman is waiting, gun holstered, as she leans on the Jeep with her arms folded.

Eve lets out a startled grumble and I step in front to shield her with my body. "What the Hell do you want?" I demand.

This time, what she pulls out is her FBI credentials, which look dishearteningly real. "We need to talk," she says firmly.

CHAPTER 13

Eve

I stand frozen, full of questions, while Michael shoves himself in front of me as if he's expecting a bullet. The look of desperation on his face only adds to my questions. Who is this woman?

"Well, I'm glad to see you're not deceased," the woman sighs. I peek around Michael and look at her badge. Carolyn Moss, FBI. And she knows Michael's full name.

That's not a good sign.

"Who are you and who am I to you?" Michael demands.

"As I said, we need to talk. Come with me and we'll get this sorted out." Her voice is rational...and peculiarly fatigued.

"Am I getting arrested?" Michael asks, and a cold stone drops into the pit of my stomach. I start to shake.

"Not at this point. However, there are some things you should know." She stays leaning on my Jeep as if she owns it, sparing me one curious glance before ignoring me again.

"Michael, who is this woman, and why would you get arrested?"

Panic is in my voice. He said his life was dangerous. Someone had tried to kill him. But this?

The woman startles slightly and blinks at me in complete confusion, as if noticing me for the first time and wondering where I came from. "This is simply routine," she says hastily, seeming apprehensive to upset me or give me the wrong impression. "Are you the owner of the car at the bottom of that hill?"

"Leave her out of this!" Michael snarls with desperation in his voice. "It's not her car."

"Then would you mind explaining why you were digging it out?" Her eyes keep flicking to Michael's forehead, where his injury just peeks out below his hairline.

"It's my rental car." Michael's voice is calm and steady. "I was in the crash alone. It gave my brains a good knock and I've been figuring out what happened ever since."

Her face falls for a moment, and then she gives him a suspicious look. "How do I know you're not handing me a line of crap?"

"Lady, I didn't even know what my last name was until I saw it on the rental forms. I've been snowed in with an injury and no chance of getting to a doctor before now. And since you don't have a thing to detain me on besides getting shot at and crashing my car—"

"Tony Lucca." The FBI agent—if that's what she actually is—stated in a deadpan voice, as if certain that it will stop him short.

Instead, it only seems to confuse Michael. "Who?"

Her eyes widen as they fix on his wound, and her face falls. "You have to be fucking kidding me! You really don't remember?"

"Barely a thing, anyway." He pushes aside his hair and she gasps.

"Okay, I'm starting to believe you. But we have a problem here. Whoever shot you is still in the area and they're looking for you. And we want them." She opens her stance slightly.

Oh. That sounds less irrational. Was Michael a witness to something? Something critical enough that criminals want him dead?

"I'd be happy to help if my fucking brains get unscrambled. As it is —" he freezes all of a sudden.

"Get down!" He grabs me and pulls me behind the Jeep's steel plow just as a bullet thuds into a tree behind us.

I let out a reflexive scream as the FBI agent whips around and pulls out a massive silver firearm. She takes partial cover behind her sedan and aims into the trees. Michael's shielding me with his body. "Just hold still, it'll be okay," he reassures me.

But it's not okay. Nothing about this is okay, and as the FBI agent exchanges gunfire with whoever's up behind the trees, I start to tremble and cry. The tears feel like ice on my cheeks, and I keep waiting for him to grunt with pain as another bullet hits him. Except this one will take him away from me.

And somehow, I'm more worried about that than about all the trouble we're in, or how I wouldn't be getting shot at if I never met him. That thought creeps into my head in a tide of panicked resentment; it's just easier to push aside.

"Damn it! There are at least two shooters," the agent growls as she ducks back down.

"Don't you have any backup?" Michael sounds astonished.

"Nope! My superior's an asshole." She sounds less hostile toward him—but more exasperated.

"Then who's the guy with the construction crew?" One of the men up the road was staring at us peculiarly, though I didn't think anything of it at the time.

All of us turn at once—in time to see one of the construction guys approaching with a pistol in his hand. It is aimed directly at the FBI agent.

The agent lets out a shriek and brings her gun toward him—and a pistol goes off right next to me, leaving my ears ringing. The guy's head flies back in a puff of red mist as he goes down, his pistol flying out of his hand.

"Jesus!" yells someone up the hill loud enough for me to hear over the ringing in my ears. The agent pops up and takes another shot that direction, and someone hollers. Then the shooting stops.

Michael is crouched over me, holding a black pistol. His dark eyes are tough with purpose. He holsters the pistol under his arm and turns to meet my astonished stare.

His face falls. "Sorry," he says quietly. "Are you okay?"

I am, and even though the risk may have been because of him—and unintentionally so—he did what had to be done. From the look of apprehension and confusion, he likely did it on instinct.

And it didn't just save the FBI agent's life. It also saved mine.

"I'm just frightened, I need my pills." I feel terribly unequipped for this situation.

"Okay," he says, crouching down to hug me, ignoring the agent for the moment. She's yelling into her phone, something about additional agents, an ambulance and local law enforcement. "It's okay. We'll get this sorted out and go home."

I sob for a few moments before get it under control. The tears chill my cheeks further, stinging. "What is all this?" I'm mumbling into his chest as he strokes my hair.

"I'm not sure," he says. "But I'll tell you what I've figured out as soon as we get out of here."

The agent hangs up her phone with a curse and turns to us. Michael looks at her. She stares back, seeming to be at a loss for words.

"You could have shot me in the back," she mutters, sounding completely astonished. "Instead you saved my life."

"Listen, lady," Michael replies hoarsely. "I know little about what is going on, but I'm not fucking with those guys. And no, I'm not going to let some asshole shoot you just because you're in my face waving a badge."

"You're not what I expected..." she hesitates. Then her expression goes cold again. "Where did you get the gun?" she demands, and I tighten my grip on his shoulder, wanting to know too.

"It was in the rental." He didn't tell me he found it, which puts a dent in my trust for him. But I'll hold out on judging until I have more facts.

"That's what you came back for?" Her gun is still out but not pointing at us.

"I came back for the suitcase, and to see what I could remember by looking at the car. I have been wearing the same clothes for two days. I came for personal belongings. I don't even know if the gun's mine." Annoyance drips from every word.

"So you won't mind if I check it for prints and registration?" Her voice isn't as cold as it was at the start, but it's implacable as she holds out a hand toward him.

"Fine." He reverses the gun and hands it to her butt first. "I doubt you'll find anything connected to me, but go ahead."

She frowns. "Seriously. You're not the guy I was expecting."

"Maybe you were expecting someone who doesn't exist?" Michael retorts. "I just want to get indoors and put an ice pack on my head."

"Fine." She fishes inside her coat for a card and holds it out. "Call me. I want to make a deal with you. Don't try and rabbit on me, I will track you down."

"Fine. Are we free to go?" Michael's voice is hard as nails.

"For now," she replies, sparing me another curious look. "But I'll expect to hear from you tomorrow."

Michael gives a resigned sigh and nods.

CHAPTER 14

Eve

I can't speak as we drive away, rushing toward town instead of home in case we're followed. Michael is driving as I shiver in the passenger seat. My ear still hurts from that gun shot.

I think he killed that man.

What choice was there? If he hadn't used the gun, would we be dead now? Or that FBI agent?

What to do? The man I'm in love with is like a hero and a monster simultaneously.

Michael speaks before I can bring myself to. "If you want, we can double back through town. I'll call a cab as soon as I get you home, and get out of your life. I would never have endangered you like that if I had known."

How much of that is true? There's a lot of quiet lust behind it. I find myself on the verge of an anxiety attack, and don't push the issue.

"I evoke more now. If I had known they put a guy in the

construction crew to watch for me, I would never have asked you to go with me. I sure wouldn't have deliberately involved you in a shootout."

"Of course not," I manage, eyes spilling over, sniffling.

He winces but keeps focused on the road. "Just...tell me how I can make this right."

My anxiety takes hold of me and I want to scream that he can't make this right, that it's too late for that. But I bite back those words and take a deep breath.

"You know, maybe the only reason I'm not telling you to get the hell out of my life is that nobody ever cared about me or wanted to make things right with me." The words spill out, and they sound senseless, but at least not full of hate.

"What do you mean? Jesus, the least I owe you is a fucking apology. You saved my life, and in return, I dragged you into danger." He hesitates, then continues. "This is my screw-up, and it's a big one."

"Yeah, it is." My voice is trembling and childish, and my eyes are streaming, blurring the road ahead into gray-white streaks. "That scared me, and I never want to go through it again."

"Me neither. I don't know what to do about my past, but wish to keep you as far away from it as possible. That's why I offered to leave." His hands are white-knuckled on the wheel. He might be a stoic, but he's hiding his own fears under his cool, grim exterior.

I wipe my eyes and look out the window at the white blur, trying not to think about how red my face is or how my nose will start running soon. "Just...commence with the truth. And yes...let's go home. I don't want to have a breakdown in public."

"I understand. I don't think the guys who shot at us will do it somewhere with street cameras." His voice has changed. It's not only full of determination but somehow implacable, like he's ready to plow through an army to get us home safe.

I just really hope it won't come to that.

"This is what I know for certain. My name's Michael Di Lorenzo. I'm Canadian, but might have been born in Italy.

"I was working for some risky men in Montreal. Mobsters, I think.

That guy Bertie was one of them. The guys who shot at us must have been his cronies.

"I had wanted out for a long time." There are long pauses between his words, as if he's still trying to figure out how much of what he's saying is real and how much is imagination. It sounds so crazy that if I hadn't been shot at ten minutes ago, I would have thought it was a product of his rattled brains.

"They wanted me to do a job at a ski lodge. I was supposed to assassinate a kid for them. A fucking kid! They must have counted on my saying no." He laughed humorlessly.

I feel sick. "A child? How...why?"

"To punish the boy's mother for running away. It was revolting, and I completely refused." We pass a fuel truck puttering down the road; ahead is the turn-off for Great Barrington.

"Anyway, Bertie knew I would never do a job like that. But he pointed a gun at me and tried to force me. He knew the boss already decided to set me up. The penalty for refusing is death, after all."

He goes quiet, and when I look at his face his brows are furrowed in concentration. He slows for the turn-off, and says, "I'm not sure I like the man I used to be, but he would have never killed a kid."

"Who did he kill then?" I can't believe I'm asking him that.

"Mobsters, that's my guess. It was a war. Our guys, and guys from other cities wanted our territory." He sighs with relief as we reach town.

It looks so ordinary right now. People are wandering around shopping, going to the tiny theater, making snowmen in their yards. I used to feel a world away from these folks, separated by something unexplainable that would keep us from being able to relate. Now I realize there are outsiders...and then there are folks so far outside normal their lives seem like an action movie.

"Bertie and I were friends for a very long time. I got him this job. In the end, he chose the profession over me."

I nod, able to look at him again and see gloom in his eyes. My heart is pounding and my chest hurts from too many bouts of distress and agony. I wish things could go back to a few hours ago when I woke up in his arms.

Instead, here I am facing a truth so ugly that I'm starting to understand how his amnesia might be from trauma after all. "This man was your best friend?" What a crappy example! The worst I ever had were gossipers and bullies. His "best friend" set him up to be executed!

"Yeah, and he pointed a gun at me. He may have set up the ambush. One of the guys must have checked on him when he didn't show up. But as soon as I drove past the turnoff to the ski resort, they were waiting for me."

"They must have realized if you didn't take the turnoff, you refused the contract. It was at the ski lodge?" This is hands down the most bizarre conversation I have ever had!

He grunts acknowledgment. "Probably. That seems about right." He shoots another furtive look at me. "Still wonder why you're not kicking me out of the Jeep. I've got the cash to look after myself now. You have no obligation to me."

He's trying to let me off the hook. Letting me know he can go away if I don't feel safe.

"I know." My shivering has stopped, and the ringing in my ears subsided. "If anything…"

I feel like I'm on thin ice. But I was on thin ice with people. That's what the damn anxiety does to me. So I push on.

"If anything, you have an obligation to me, Michael Di Lorenzo." I can't even speak after getting that sentence out; panic wells up in me!

"I agree," he says in a temperate voice. "It is up to you to tell me how to repay you."

He's been bouncing around the subject, only being direct a few times. Maybe he doesn't remember the full extent of the truth? It doesn't change the fact that I'm in love with a man who's trying to make a clean break from the mob.

So much damn anxiety, I can barely handle more than a few hours around anyone without becoming exhausted! And yet he's possibly been through a thousand times worse!

Maybe the bullet wound was incidental? Something in his mind used that as an excuse to chuck his old self—everything... The past doesn't vanish because you choose to forget about it!

"Tell me the rest of what you know." My voice is no longer a trembling, embarrassing muddle. That's a good sign.

"No one is back home, because the only thing I regretted leaving behind was my condo in Montreal and my art collection. I was thinking about it when the ambush happened. If there was...someone...I would have been thinking about her instead."

"That's good to know." I laugh nervously. "You were already in Massachusetts when Bertie caught up with you, right?"

"I must have been. I was here for someone else. The target was a thug, not a kid."

He stops at the light and we watch a line of brightly-bundled children follow a woman through the crosswalk like ducklings. A man follows behind, surreptitiously, as if even he has trouble keeping track of how many kids he has. Michael smiles.

"I always liked kids and animals. I think it pissed my bosses off sometimes. No innocents. Especially no kids. Just combatants like me who knew what they were in for."

One of the little ones slips halfway across the street and we both tense, but her dad lunges forward and catches her. "How did your boss catch on that you wanted to leave?"

"Maybe I confided in Bertie?" The crosswalk clears; the light changes, and he starts forward again.

"I don't know how to feel about this." This man, who has been nothing but kind to me, also killed someone right in front of me? It's even harder to grasp that slaying people was his job.

"I'm just grateful that you're still talking to me." His voice gets a grim note, despite the rawness of his statement. "Why are you still putting up with me?"

"Because it's not putting up with! You're the first to give a damn about me. You don't scare me, even knowing what you can do—what you did." The words are spilling out, and I can't stop them. I only manage to keep the desperation out of my voice.

"I dealt with a lot growing up, Michael, and thanks to my brain chemistry, it was tougher. These days, no one around me can be trusted.

"And yet I trust you. There has to be a reason. I'm not completely irrational. In fact, it goes the other direction." My voice fills with cynicism.

"You're the only person I've actually wanted to be around in over ten years."

"Even...knowing?" He sounds astonished.

"Yes," I admit it to myself as much as him. "Even knowing that you used to kill mobsters for a living."

He drives quietly the rest of the way. We're swinging back onto the Interstate back home, before he speaks up again. "Now, I'm not sure how to feel. But that's mostly because I might not deserve you."

"Nobody's ever said that to me," I sigh, heart mired in the past, depression settling over me like a heavy blanket of snow. I shake some of it off and press on. "Do you recollect anything else?"

"Yes, I took the gun away from Bertie, his phone, and whacked him across the head. And..." He frowns. "I don't remember the crash still, but remember following the Interstate and then going up the hill to your lights."

"The two men?" What was it like? Slogging through the cold night with a head wound, with only the glow of a distant porch light to offer him any hope of survival.

"I must have killed them. The car, my gun. It hasn't made the news, so they're probably going to find the bodies when the snow melts." He winces. "Yet another reason why I should probably leave and take further trouble away from you."

"It's too late." Not just because I love him and let him become my lover. "It's a small town. They'll know where I live soon enough. The FBI agent undoubtedly has my location by now."

I close my eyes on sudden tears. I can't stand this. It isn't fair. He's inadvertently brought danger and uncertainty into my life.

"I'm sorry," he whispers, pain and guilt thick in his tone. "But I still want to find a way to make this right."

"Then leaving isn't an option right now. Don't just dump all this on me and run. I hate that. My father did it." I hate even thinking about the sperm donor, whose careless actions damned me nearly as much as my mother's abusive ones.

"What do you mean? I don't know much about your past!" He adds quickly, "If you feel like talking about it..."

"It's fine. Quid pro quo, I guess." Where to start?

I plow into it. "My dad got my mom pregnant and took off as soon as he found out. He said because she was too fat. She took that out on me. So I was in disarray before I even started school. All those shitty classmates smelled blood in the water and pounced.

"It broke me down. Kids without good parenting are cruel, and so when I showed up in the schoolyard dragging a broken wing, they saw an easy target." Fucking miniature monsters.

I remember those moments mostly as rings of faces, stolen books, mocking voices. Why was everyone so vicious to me? It thrilled them to be so, and I was the target because I was too broken to fight back.

"It just went on like that. Some asshole damage to me, so then another asshole sees I'm an easy target and does more harm. And on and on like that. Then I started dating and...It was dreadful."

"Most young guys are awful, honey, you don't even have to tell me." The highway's almost clear, with only a few cars to compete with us for position on the road. "You're a sensitive soul and you got shit on. I get it now.

"I would rather stay here and protect you than do anything else," he admits in a rush, and my heart leaps and starts beating faster. "But first I got to figure out how to get rid of the men after me."

"After us," I remind firmly.

He nods. "Yeah, after us. I should start by seeing what's in the damn suitcase."

CHAPTER 15

Michael

The suitcase has a false bottom. That's why it's so heavy.

It's has little out of the ordinary inside. Some ski clothes and snow boots, two changes of clothes, and a bag of toiletries.

I have to search for five minutes to find the catch for the false bottom. Amnesia is such a pain in the ass!

Eve watches anxiously as we sit on the sofa, the suitcase laid out on the timber coffee table in front of us. Freya has already hopped into the other half of the suitcase and is curled up on my snowsuit. Even Diogenes is perched on the edge of the suitcase, peering at me as if trying to figure out what I'm doing.

Finally I find the catch under the layer of liner fabric and twist it; there's a click, and the false bottom pops open. I grab the edge and swing it wide, and stare at what was hidden inside.

"Well shit," I mutter as Eve gasps.

A small box with several straps of cash, some exotic-looking electronics including a shotgun microphone for long-distance spying, and a safe deposit box key. Next to it is a heavily padded gun case. I stare at the broken-down sniper rifle and ammunition inside, with its long, heavy silencer and flash suppressor.

Diogenes flaps his little chicken wings. "More dakka!"

"Yeah," I mutter. "Something like that."

"What were you planning to do with that?"

"I don't know." I feel a little sick. "Miss FBI Agent can probably tell me."

"You have to call her, don't you?" she sounds scared and gloomy, and I wrap a comforting arm around her.

"Yes. I don't know if she's really willing to leave me alone if I give up the others, but if she's willing to arrange a deal to leave us in peace... I have to try..."

She nods, and leans over for a kiss. I give it gladly, hoping it won't be our last.

We visit the urgent care center before I deal with the Fed. They check me over, give me a scrip for more painkillers and send me on my way. No permanent damage. That is a relief.

Then why hasn't the rest of my memory returned?

Eve sits beside me as I make the call. "This is Michael Di Lorenzo," I say when she picks up. "We need to talk."

"Yes, we absolutely do." Her voice is all business, hiding any surprise. "Amnesiac or not, you're a suspect in a recent murder in the United States. Not to mention the one you committed right in front of me."

My eyes narrow. Audacious bitch! "You mean when I saved your life?"

There's a pause. "The fact that you saved my life is the only reason you didn't end that encounter in handcuffs. You and your accomplice."

My blood boils at the implication. "She's my girlfriend, not my accomplice. You want to threaten innocent people with arrests?" I look at Eve and see how scared she is, and snarl "Don't bully her because you want me. Or the guys after me, for that matter."

"I want you," she snaps. "But I'll take them."

"And you can have them. I'll even be willing to use myself as bait. In return for that and my testifying, you leave me—and especially Eve—alone." My voice is stony. Right now I'm half tempted to put together that sniper rifle and hunt for her instead!

"If you can deliver whoever's left in the area, and are willing to testify, we have a deal. Otherwise, forget about it." She waits for my reply.

"I'll set it up. Get some backup and wait for my call." A cold confidence has settled into me. My consciousness might not remember that I'm on familiar ground, but the rest of me does.

I hang up, and then go through my phone some more. I find Bertie's phone number. He has two entries. The second one picks up.

"Mikey, you have a lot of goddamn nerve calling me after the shit you pulled," he starts growling. "You broke my goddamn nose!"

"Better than breaking your skull. I can still come back and do it the other way." And just talking to him makes me want to do it!

"The boss is real pissed off, Mikey. You can't just leave. That's not how things work."

"Because I'm not going back to Canada? I'm never doing another job! Call me retired, Bertie. My only mistake was talking to you about it instead of just walking away."

"No, your mistake was refusing the job." He sounds fuming.

"What have you become, Bertie?" I snap. "What the Hell do you think I've become? Since when are you okay with killing kids?"

Eve makes a small sound of discomfort and I reach over and squeeze her hand reassuringly.

Bertie hesitates. For a moment, something in me remembers my cousin and my friend hopes. It's not okay. He's being forced too. Just that bit of unwillingness. It's all it would take to forgive him—at least a little.

"Since when am I okay with it? Since the Boss offered us ten million to split to get it done? Turns out that woman is his. She's one of his most valuable pieces of property." He says this casually as if he's talking about a bet on a horse.

Oh, you absolute turd. "Then the kid is probably his!"

"Call it a retroactive abortion."

My back teeth hurt from grinding them. I know what to do! "We need to meet," I say. "Talk about this face to face."

This time I can practically hear the wheels turning in his head. "Okay, fine, we can do that. I need some lead time to get back into town. How about the far end of the lodge parking lot this evening at nine?"

"I'll be there." I hang up, feeling sick.

Eve sees the look on my face and walks up to hug me. "Is it bad?"

"He's done," I sigh. "There's nothing left of my old friend. There will be no problem giving him up."

I call the FBI agent back up and we make the arrangements. And around eight that night, I kiss Eve goodbye and tell her to wait for me as I put the sniper rifle together.

"You'll be back, right?" she looks at me with sad eyes and I almost can't walk out the door.

"I promise."

I take her Jeep past the entrance, sling the rifle and hike up onto the low ridge overlooking the lot. I climb up a tree and set up my makeshift sniper's nest, and wait with the headphones for the shotgun mic over my ears and the device on, aimed at the meet spot.

I see several nondescript-looking sedans show up. Men get out and disperse among the parked cars near that corner. Men...and one woman, who gets out of a dark blue sedan with her braid flashing almost silver in the semi-dark.

Ten minutes later, another set of dark sedans arrive. They park closer to the meet spot; at least six goons aside from Bertie, who looks annoyed when he sees I'm not waiting for him.

"You guys spread out," he tells the others. I aim the rifle and see his scowl through the scope. "That prick better not have chickened out!"

My finger settles on the trigger briefly as I'm tempted. But I have worse in store for him than a quick death. I remove it, watch, and listen.

A few moments later, he pulls out his phone and dials me. I turn off the mic and answer the buzzing device.

"Where the fuck are you?" he demands.

"Close enough that I can see you still haven't learned to adjust a tie properly, Captain Clip-On."

He spins around nervously. "You're in the parking lot?"

"I'm on my way. Sit tight."

He smiles broadly, his voice going warm and reasonable and full of lies. "Hey, however you want to play it. You've been a loyal hitter, cousin. The Boss will let you go if you ask nicely enough."

"You mean if I go back with you?" The shake in my voice is from suppressed laughter, but it sounds like nervousness.

"Yeah. Just come over and we'll work it out." He glances over at one of the cars; A guy in the front seat rack has a good round on his shotgun.

"Sure, be right there." I hang up and call the agent again. "Are you in place?"

"How many did you count?" Her voice has a steely calm that makes me glad she decided to offer the deal. I couldn't shake her without killing her otherwise—and I couldn't come home and explain that to Eve.

"Six. At least one has a shotgun. All of them are armed. You have enough guys for that?" She's a lot easier to talk to now that we're on the same side. "We'll manage. Where are you?" She sounds a bit wary.

"Making sure you live long enough to collect on our bargain. Better grab them fast, Bertie's always been unreasonable." Except with me. He still somehow trusts me to show up and keep my end, even after betraying me.

Idiot.

"Got it. Talk soon." She hangs up, and I put my headphones back on and aim the mic at Bertrand.

Here it comes, you bastard.

The look on his face when a dozen FBI agents pour out from

behind cars and from a van almost makes up for the shit he's put me through.

The mobsters burst out to back him up as Special Agent Moss approaches with gun drawn and her men close in too. Suddenly everyone's pointing guns at everyone else...and I'm suddenly at a loss for who to point mine at first!

I hated cops! But I don't want trouble, and I hate Bertie even more now. Him and all his kind. So I guess I'm going back to my old job one last time:

Shooting mobsters!

Bertie spins around to aim his gun at Moss, who fires and misses. In that split second, I have a target.

I pull the trigger, and Bertie folds up and goes down, dropping his gun and holding himself. He yells, curses at the top of his lungs as the other agents swarm in to arrest his backup.

Moss calls me again. "You shot him through the buttocks!"

"Biggest target," I say, deadpan, and she lets out an incredulous laugh as she pulls out her handcuffs. "Besides, he can't sing about his boss to the Canadians if he's dead."

"That he can't." She sounds almost giddy. "You know, I'll trade one mob hitter for seven any day. Pleasure doing business with you."

"Just remember your promise," I remind her. "You're to leave us alone now unless you need a witness."

"Or a bodyguard! Holy shit." She locks the cuffs on the still nonstop bitching Bertrand and then straightens and steps away so her men can deal with him.

"I'm already guarding someone full time," I say quietly.

She stops, her voice is quite a bit gentler when she speaks again. "The redhead?"

"Yes," I sigh. Admitting it to someone brings me a strange sense of peace. "I'm needed there. I'll fucking die before I leave her side for longer than a court case. Not that I expect you to understand."

A sad, wistful look on her face, one that I never thought I could possibly see there. "You'd be surprised," she says unobtrusively. "We're done here. Keep this phone in case I need to call you."

"I will."

It's freezing and a few flakes are falling again, but I stay there, watching as every single last one of the men sent to kill me end up handcuffed and stuffed into the van. An ambulance comes for Bertie, who's still bitching in three languages as they load him in. He can't believe I did him like this.

"Fuck you, Bertie," I mutter as I break down my gear. "One good betrayal deserves another."

The snow's falling fast by the time I drive the Jeep up onto Eve's land and secure it in the garage. I leave the rifle in the back seat. She's asked me not to bring it in the house until she's more used it.

As I walk through the snow, the memory of my first walk up the hill comes flooding back: freezing, legs made of lead, head stinging and cold from the blood dripping off of it. Are those lights ahead? Who's home? Can I trust them?

As it turned out, I could trust Eve, and I can. With my life, my secrets...and my heart.

This time, I don't fall short when I make my way up onto the porch. I walk up to the door instead and knock.

Eve runs to the door and pulls it open—and is a trembling, sobbing bundle in my arms before I can say hello. This time, I'm the one who carries her inside.

"Is it over?" she asks a while later, cried out and curled up on my lap on the couch.

"Yeah," I say. I've told her everything—including the deal I made. "If any of the Sixth Family's men come sniffing through these hills looking for trouble, I still have the rifle and I'm better. I'll make it too costly for my old boss to keep sending men. Every last one of them will be shot or arrested."

"So you'll keep working with the FBI lady?" She looks at me and I thumb the tear-streaks off her cheeks. Apparently she cries when she's relieved enough, too.

"I doubt she'll complain about the drive to pick up more scumbags and get credit for collaring them," I say confidently. Who would? It's clear this agent is not only unconventional, but ambitious as well.

Good thing she has a code of her own!

"It will draw too much attention if dead mobsters keep turning up." She lays her head on my shoulder as Freya jumps to join the cuddle pile.

"Yeah, and we can probably only fit a half dozen or so under the garden," I muse.

She gives me a Look. "Michael."

I laugh and nuzzle the top of her head before kissing it. "Just kidding, sweetheart. I love you. Also, I don't want the tomatoes to taste funny."

"I love you too. And no bodies in the garden!"

We both laugh, and I close my eyes and lean back. I still have foggy memories and my millions to retrieve from a safe deposit box, and there may still be more. But all of that doesn't matter right now.

It's enough that I'm home, safe in this snug and private place, with Eve!

EPILOGUE

Carolyn

"I can't believe it. You couldn't find Di Lorenzo, so instead you brought me back every single damn mobster that was after him? How did you manage?" For the first time since I told him to go back to his wife and stop hitting on me, AD Derek Daniels is staring at me in amazement.

It's all I can do to keep my professional composure. I want to gloat. Seven collars in a single hour, with nobody hurt—except for Bertrand Blanc, of course. "Yes sir. I figured that even if they got to Di Lorenzo, which it looks like they did, I could still grab us a bunch of Sixth Family operatives."

He nods slowly, actually looking impressed. "Not bad. But you didn't answer my question."

"I conned Bertrand into thinking Di Lorenzo was still alive, instead of at the crash site with his face shot off. They wanted him dead and he's dangerous, so they brought all their guys in the area. Then we just grabbed them."

"And you're sure the guy you exchanged fire with, the one dressed as a construction worker—you're sure he was Di Lorenzo?" He's fiddling with things on his desk, probably nervous because he doesn't have anything to bitch at me about.

"I was firing from cover, I never got a clear look at his face until he didn't have one. But he's the right height, build and hair color, and ambushing from disguise is one of his common tactics." I know that guy wasn't Di Lorenzo, of course, but since we don't have fingerprints, DNA or dental records on file, there's no way of telling that.

Di Lorenzo didn't ask me to fake his death so that no other agent would go looking for him and probably get themselves shot. It was my idea. Partly because a deal's a deal—and partly because he saved my life. Twice.

Maybe Prometheus was right to want him out of jail and keeping watch over some shy Massachusetts art geek instead.

"Just one thing," he says as he closes the file in front of him. "Why did you shoot Blank through the butt-cheeks?"

"He was aiming at Rogers while Rogers was busy handcuffing one of his men. It was the largest non-lethal target available." I say it deadpan.

He snorts and has to struggle with laughter for a moment. "Very professional."

"Thank you, sir."

He shakes his head. "Yeah, well, I'll recommend you for a bonus. But I'm only giving you till the end of the weekend off. We have three more men on our list, after all."

I nod, keeping my triumphant smile off my face until I have a chance to walk out. "Yes sir. I'll be ready."

"Fine, get out of here. I gotta go attend Lucca's trial." He waves me off, and I turn and go, headed for the exit.

Once I'm safely in my car, I let out a yell of triumph and pound the steering wheel. A few seconds later, my phone beeps. It's a message from an unknown caller.

Well done, Carolyn. You have arrested seven wicked men, and given a good man a chance to be good once again.

I frown, texting my answer. **Why did you want to keep him out of prison?**

A brief pause. **Because the justice system is broken. It no longer does justice 90% of the time. This must be corrected.**

I sit back, thinking about that. That frightened red-haired girl I saw cowered behind Di Lorenzo like she was scared of the whole world. Maybe she does need him by her side more than I need revenge for losing Lucca.

Especially since I now know he did it on the Sixth Family's orders while he was trying to escape the life. And most especially because letting him go netted me seven others.

Sometimes the road to real justice has some seriously strange bends in it, I acknowledge finally.

Exactly. Now, get some rest, you've been neglecting yourself again. I'll get back in touch soon.

I take a deep breath and ask a final question. **Are you ever going to tell me who you are?**

Another pause. **Don't worry, Carolyn. We will meet soon enough.**

He blocks my number, leaving me even more curious than before. Who is this Prometheus? And why is he so interested in me?

Time will tell.

THE END.

❀ Created with Vellum

CPSIA information can be obtained
at www.ICGtesting.com
Printed in the USA
BVHW041406100221
599801BV00005B/122

9 781648 087875